Y0-AET-719

STAR
OF THE SEA

Star of the Sea

LINDA HALDEMAN

DOUBLEDAY & COMPANY, INC.

GARDEN CITY, NEW YORK

1978

Lines from "A Psalm" by Thomas Merton reprinted from Thomas Merton, *Collected Poems*. Copyright 1949 by Our Lady of Gethsemani Monastery, copyright © 1977 by The Trustees of the Merton Legacy Trust. Reprinted by permission of New Directions Publishing Corporation.

Lyrics from "We're Off to See the Wizard" and "Follow the Yellow Brick Road" by E. Y. Harburg and Harold Arlen copyright © 1939, renewed 1967 by Leo Reist, Inc. Reprinted by permission.

Library of Congress Cataloging in Publication Data

Haldeman, Linda.
Star of the Sea.

I. Title.
PZ4.H1615St [PS3558.A354] 813'.5'4
ISBN: 0-385-13363-4
Library of Congress Catalog Card Number 77–82759

Copyright © 1978 by Linda Haldeman
All Rights Reserved
Printed in the United States of America
First Edition

2

All of the characters in this book are fictitious,
and any resemblance to actual persons, living or dead,
is purely coincidental.

In affectionate memory of my parents.

STAR
OF THE SEA

I

THE WAR had been over for five years, and world peace still seemed a blessed reality to those who did not listen too closely to the news from Central Europe and the East. April had been going on for some time, and spring was already showing signs of maturing into murky subtropic summer. The town of Frenchmen's Bay, Mississippi, stretched in full bloom along the shore of a small inlet off the Gulf of Mexico. The crescent of landscaped estates along the beach, lavish imitations of ante-bellum plantation houses occasionally interrupted by something startlingly Spanish in stucco, blushed pink and delicate with beds of azaleas, lilies and late-blooming hyacinths. Gigantic white blossoms smelling strongly of frangipani decorated the two large magnolia trees in front of the whitewashed brick façade of the Convent of the Holy Innocents. There were no flowers, however, only pavement for parking, in front of the large red brick building located conveniently next to the convent—the parish church of Our Lady, Star of the Sea.

The town proper, the markets and banks and offices, existed in quiet contentment a quarter of a mile or so inland from the beach. It was a typical southern town, pretty, bourgeois and conservative, the site of small, neatly painted houses surrounded by carefully tended yards and almost inevitably protected from the dubious compliments of stray dogs by chain link fences. No trace here of memories of France or Spain. The Methodist church stood solid and complacent, looking with approval upon the modest prosperity and diligent virtue surrounding it, pointedly ignoring the foreign extravagance of the Catholic church and scarcely aware of the little Episcopal mission hiding embarrassed on a side street.

Another quarter mile back was the abode of the poor, carefully hidden from the sight of visitors and prosperous townspeople alike. Here were mostly frame shotgun houses with one shabby square room leading into the next, the lawns rusty junkyards where eviscerated Fords crowded decrepit but tenanted chicken coops and hound kennels. The less fortunate residents of Frenchmen's Bay, most of them black, managed with dirt roads and unpainted cabins. Their gardens produced food and were fertilized by outhouses. One square frame building, little larger than a storeroom, stood out, for it glistened with recently applied whitewash. On the front of the building above the door a large brilliant pink valentine had been painted; below it carefully made block letters of the same iridescent pink declared in cheery optimism: "Harts of Love Baptist Church No. 2."

It was a comfortable town to be a policeman in, for nothing much happened. That is one reason Giuseppe Verdi Palmisano was on the force. He was a gentle man, adept at directing traffic during May processions and homecoming parades, a master at reassuring lost children and cooling down Saturday night quarrels. But he was incapable of violence, and although he carried a service revolver and knew how to use it, he probably would have been killed in any actual gunfight before he could bring himself to fire upon a fellow creature.

He was on the desk Wednesday night and took the call.

"This is Guinevere Simpson," a high, thin voice said. Giuseppe thought at first that it was the voice of a child, but both the content of her message and the calm efficiency with which she delivered it caused him to doubt that.

"Sylvia has cut her wrists. I've bandaged her up but she won't come to. Maybe you'd better send an ambulance. The address is Number Twenty-one West Beach Drive. Thank you."

Before Giuseppe could respond the caller hung up. Half dazed, he wrote out the address and called the rescue detail. There, it was out of his hands now. But it was not so easily out of his mind. He could have sworn it was the voice of a child—and as the father of nine noisy children, he ought to know. He nervously doodled on the blank pad in front of him, wrote the word "child" and decorated it, putting curly hair on the "c," drawing a frightened face on the "d." Annoyed, he crossed the word out, obliterating it under heavy lines. He had no business allowing himself to get involved. Anyway, it probably wasn't a child at all. An old lady, maybe even an old man. Then he chuckled, comforted by a new amusing conjecture. It was probably some kind of a hoax, a silly teen-ager calling to ask if they had Prince Albert in a can. The phone began ringing again and Giuseppe returned to his proper work, dismissing the matter as settled.

It was the repetition of the word "child" that startled him into recalling the incident. Thursday evening before work he sat with a few of his fellows at the corner table in Annie's Lunch drinking a great mug of strong, black, chicory-laced coffee. The corner table was the Cops' Table, respectfully reserved by the locals for the use of the officers from the station house across the street. A young, fair-haired rooky was entertaining the table with a wild tale about a call he had gone out on the night before.

"You should have seen the place, all marble and mirrors and those dinky little chairs that look like they'll bust if you sneeze at them. And here was this child, a little kid, maybe nine or ten, standing in the middle of this marble hall wrapped in one of them Chinese robes, what-do-you-call—kimonos. Looked like real silk.

" 'She's upstairs,' the kid says, just like that, cool as a cucumber. I wish my wife could've seen that bathroom! It was marble too, or something like marble. Even the flusher was gold. And there's this woman lying right in the middle of the floor, out cold.

" 'I don't think she's in any real danger,' the kid says. 'I came right away when I heard something fall. She always knocks stuff over so she'll be found before she really hurts herself. I was afraid there'd be trouble. They had a real bad fight, her and Tony. And they'd been drinking a lot.'

"That was putting it mildly. The old girl smelled like a still."

"Was the child alone?" Giuseppe asked anxiously.

"She said she wasn't. Somebody named Maud was asleep in another bedroom. The kid said there was no use trying to wake her because she took medicine. And there was some kind of maid or cook asleep downstairs. I asked the kid if the woman on the floor was her mother. She frowned like she wasn't sure. 'Yes,' she said slowly, like she'd never thought about it before. 'Yes. Right. She's my mother.'

"I took a look at Maud. The kid thinks she's her grandmother. That one was sure feeling no pain. The room was full of pill bottles and stuff. All legal, of course, prescriptions and like that. I didn't have a search warrant so there was nothing to do there. I made sure the cook was sane and sober, and the kid went back to bed, as calm as you please. I hated to leave her there, but what can you do? Goddamn mink-lined loony bin, that's what it was." He downed his coffee in one vociferous gulp.

Giuseppe stared gloomily into his own half-empty cup. The coffee had gone cold and developed a greasy look. His finger absent-mindedly traced on the shiny black table surface the word "child."

2

Friday Morning, just past eleven, all classes were in session at Holy Innocents Academy. Monsignor Fulham, pastor of Star of the Sea, was putting the current First Communion class through its final preparations. Catechism was satisfactory, at least as satisfactory as Catechism can ever be as a means of making acquaintance with the Unknowable.

"Why did God make you, Barbara?" he asked, furtively consulting the teacher's attendance chart to be sure he had associated the right name with the right face.

"God made me to know, love and serve Him here on earth and to be happy with Him forever in heaven," a confident voice chanted back.

Monsignor Fulham smiled. "Very good, Barbara," he said in the same reflective chant and searched down the list for another name to which his memory could supply a face.

Across the dusty yard from the proud new brick elementary annex hovered in rickety splendor the rambling nineteenth-century white frame convent. The secondary classes, both junior and senior high, shared the ample second floor with the administrative offices and the nuns' chapel. In the rear corner classroom overlooking the yard Sister Anne-Marie was

5

telling her seventh graders stories about St. Therese, the Little Flower. She was a good saint for seventh graders, a simple, unassuming person whom the Church wisely honored for having done all her small works for the love of God. She served as a comforting reminder to the anxious and scrupulous adolescent that small works are as acceptable to God as great ones. But gentle, unprepossessing virtues do not make good copy. So it is that stories about saints like the Little Flower tend to expand like warm dough.

"When St. Therese was a little girl," Sister Anne-Marie said, "one night when her father came into her room to tell her good-night she pretended to be asleep. Then she ran out after him to tell him that she was really awake."

"Why did she do that?" a voice floated up from somewhere in the rear of the classroom. "Is it a sin to pretend you're asleep?"

"Well, no, not really," Sister Anne-Marie interposed, anxious, somewhat belatedly, to forestall an epidemic of long-winded girlish confessions of trivial deceits.

"Oh yes, Sister," interrupted a sallow-faced, nervous girl, the sort who seemed to be willfully outgrowing everything on and around her in an effort to reach maturity before everyone else. "It's a sin against the Eighth Commandment—it's a lie."

She gave those about her a close-lipped superior smile, making certain that they realized that she had outgrown them all.

"If it is a sin," said Sister Anne-Marie, "I am sure it is a venial one."

She was greatly provoked with herself for relating such a silly anecdote. Seventh graders were a touchy lot, uncomfortably straddling the barbed fence of puberty, not yet capable of fastening their own brassieres. She often felt it her greatest duty simply to avoid contributing to their difficulties. She quickly searched her memory for a suitable saint to draw their thoughts away as far as possible from the Ten Commandments before they got into one of those awful controversies such as whether it was permissible to put one's hair in curlers on Sunday. They were too young to appreciate the

6

loose life St. Augustine had denounced and too old to be impressed by the showy exploits of some of the more colorful martyrs. Besides, the stomachs of adolescent girls were as delicate as their consciences, and the mere suggestion of the beasts of the arena or the commonplaces of the torture chamber would destroy the collective appetite of her charges for most of the day. She remembered too well the Lenten meditation in which Father Kelly's attempt to bring the class to a proper appreciation of their redemption by describing in realistic detail some of the more horrific aspects of death by crucifixion had effectively vacated the intermediate table in the refectory for two consecutive meals. With the approach of lunchtime in mind Sister Anne-Marie decided on St. Thomas Aquinas, the obese wise man of Scholasticism, who did nothing but think and eat, both with great genius, until his writings filled the library and his bulk filled the refectory to such an extent that the dining table had to be cut to fit him. Now here was a saint to be reckoned with.

Across the hall in the senior homeroom overlooking the convent's classic front veranda and giving a splendid view of the sunlit bay framed by magnolia branches and delicately crocheted hangings of Spanish moss, Father Kelly was conducting his weekly religion class. Father Kelly was young and slight of build, blessed with a cockeyed smile and an overdose of black curls. Most of the senior girls were chastely in love with him. They listened demurely, hands folded, to his anxious exhortations on behalf of virginal purity followed in due time by fecund monogamy. Sister Helen, who usually supervised this class, sat at a rear desk, her arms folded over her starched bib, a slight, ironic smile skirting her face. In deference to Father Kelly's sex and vocation the class was to be spared for one session the usual discussions of such important matters as the exact geographical boundary on the human body which separates comparatively innocent necking from potentially dangerous petting, or another hot debate on the question of whether or not the Blessed Virgin suffered labor pains when giving

7

birth to the Son of God. Teaching religion to senior girls was one of the crosses Sister Helen had to bear.

Having fulfilled his catechetical obligations, Monsignor Fulham gave the First Communion class final, practical instructions. As with all other human affairs of a formal nature, there was a code of etiquette to be observed at the altar rail—a sort of Eucharistic table manners. One ought to kneel upright, hands properly folded—straight out like a steeple, not clasped —head upraised, mouth wide open, tongue protruding slightly to receive the Host. That was a hard one to get past seven-year-olds, to whom a protruding tongue had only one significance.

"What does the Host taste like?" Someone always asked that.

"Manny says It tastes like newspaper," Aida Palmisano shouted out proudly.

Monsignor Fulham sighed. Every First Communion class since he had come to Star of the Sea had contained a precocious little Palmisano with an impossible operatic name who always managed to supply the class with an untoppable curtain line. Alfredo last year, Aida this, with Tosca and Figaro waiting in the wings.

At the other end of the elementary annex Sister Stephanie was, as usual, scolding the fifth grade. Sister Stephanie was French: wholly, desperately, fanatically French. Although she had been sent to America from the novitiate and had no prospect of ever returning to her native country, she had never become reconciled to her exile and had never completely given up hope of a recall. Her one consolation was to preach endlessly against the wickedness of the raw, young land and the certain disaster to be reaped from treating the offspring of such an unruly society with any degree of lenience. Although the fifth graders had little patience with Sister Stephanie's railings, they always experienced a certain thrill of vicarious masochism whenever she launched into the subject of discipline. If this were a French school, she delighted to tell them and they delighted to hear, they would not expiate their offenses by writing hundreds of lines or sitting out recesses in an empty classroom. Oh no, their rebellious flesh would feel the rod, an experience which Sister Stephanie enjoyed describing in detail and which her students enjoyed imagining. But in their desire not to be outdone, especially by unknown foreign students, they then responded by assuring Sister Stephanie of the brutality with which their own parents regularly beat them. This recital invariably degenerated into a contest amongst the girls, each seeking to prove her parents the most sadistic. Today it was Jennie Freret, who won by declaring that her mother used a riding crop and she had welts to prove it. No one contested her claim or demanded that she reveal her proof; the circumstantial evidence was considered sufficient. For Jennie Freret's parents owned the local riding stable and Jennie herself, an incorrigible tomboy, was reputedly the naughtiest girl in the fifth grade. Besides, she was a Protestant.

A carefully kept path bordered by perfectly matched round stones bisected the rear of the convent, separating the sports field on the left from the elementary playground on the right, disappearing at last into a thick green growth of tropical shrubbery. Half hidden in this jungle stood the old brick washhouse where Sister Lucy, who knew God with the mind of a five-year-old, was cheerfully starching blue uniform blouses and white wimples. At the end of the path, effectively isolated from the commerce of classroom and playground by the dense grove of trees and bushes, was the Shrine. According to firmly believed local legend, the Shrine rested on a spot where a landing party from Bienville's company of Canadian explorers had built a crude altar to God's Holy Mother in thanksgiving for their safe delivery from the perils of the high seas. The present Shrine was a charming little gazebo affair surrounded in a circle by the conclusion of the stone-bordered path, in the center of a carefully tended handkerchief of garden. Under the summer house roof, majestically alone, stood a wholly conventional blue-veiled statue—not the tender Madonna smiling in motherly indulgence on her Divine Infant, but the Virgin of the Immaculate Conception, beautiful in her simplicity, yet unapproachable in the very brilliance of her purity. Like an aged vestal, Sister Clementine puttered constantly about the Shrine and its garden. She had been gradually retired from her teaching duties, for she was approaching her dotage. Her devotion to the Shrine had simplified the problem of tactfully removing her from the faculty. She was named Custodian of the Shrine, a position which she now filled with admirable zeal. The enthusiasm with which she had once drilled French idioms into the recalcitrant heads of high school students she now employed against the onslaught of weeds, termites and mildew. She spent her time begging, cajoling and bargaining from all who possessed it money to add to her growing private fund for the replacement of the aging and weatherworn statue. She was rather out of sorts this morning because she couldn't find Joseph. He ought to be here to loosen dirt around the azaleas. Petulantly pulling dead blossoms from the bushes, she complained about the absent Joseph in a loud monotonous voice. She did not, as most of the students believed, talk to herself. It was to her Blessed Mother, who for Sister Clementine dwelt in reality as well as in spirit in the Shrine dedicated to her purity, that the Custodian of the Shrine berated Joseph for not being around when she needed him. Evidently the Blessed Mother did not bother to remind Sister Clementine that since the aforementioned Joseph was not a servant or even an employee of the convent, but a volunteer worker, he was free to come and go as he chose. In fact, this Joseph was the same Giuseppe Verdi Palmisano who had answered the phone at the police station. He made it his habit when off duty to lend the sisters a hand with some of the heavy labor around the convent. He received no payment for his efforts other than the sisters' gratitude and prayers. However, by some coincidence the usually efficient finance office of the school consistently forgot to bill him for the tuition of his numerous children.

While Sister Clementine waited and grumbled, Giuseppe was standing before the full but carefully organized desk of Mother Mary Ignatius, Superior of the Convent of the Holy

10

Innocents. Although frequently invited to, he never sat in Mother Ignatius' presence. He possessed a deep reverence both for the office she held and for her as a person. But anxiety and enthusiasm had now somewhat tempered his deference. The subject of his concern was the child who had called the police two nights before. He described the incident and its aftermath carefully and dramatically, drawing on his inborn sense of the theatrical to strengthen his case. It was a performance that might have drawn a tear from many a sophisticated eye. But Mother Ignatius sat immobile, her elbows resting on her ink blotter, the tips of her slim, noticeably clean fingers touching to form a peaked roof, her opaquely unreadable eyes looking directly at and yet undeniably through Giuseppe.

When he had finished telling his tale, Giuseppe stood waiting for his audience's response. The silence continued for an uncomfortably long period. At last Mother Ignatius lowered her eyes and nodded her head.

"I see, I see," she said in her low, well-controlled voice, a voice so remarkable in its leashed power that according to gossip around the convent, her whisper could silence the refectory in full shout. "We shall have to see what can be done for this child, shall we not, Mr. Palmisano?"

Her mouth moved slightly in the promise of a smile as she rose, indicating that the interview was over.

"Yes, Mother. Thank you, Mother." Giuseppe answered her smile with a broad grin of his own as he backed out of the office as though leaving the presence of royalty. He almost danced down the ponderous wooden stairs to the paved ground floor commonly referred to in that cellarless land as the "basement." He knew Mother Ignatius well enough to realize that he had won a victory. He rejoiced in that, for he loved all people's children almost as much as he loved his own; he rejoiced as well in the unexpected bounty of the superior's smile. Mother Ignatius was a splendid and saintly being (he never thought of her as a woman). She was the only adult who called him Mr. Palmisano.

Looking out her office window, Mother Ignatius spied

11

Monsignor Fulham crossing the school yard with the taste of newspaper in his mouth.

"Could I trouble you for a moment, Monsignor?" she called in an intimate voice that sounded to him as if she were beside him. Monsignor Fulham smiled as he turned back toward the convent. There could be no better antidote for a rough hour with the First Communion class than to be troubled by Mother Ignatius.

IT WAS NOON and the Angelus was starting to ring. As he once more began the journey from convent to rectory, Monsignor Fulham automatically crossed himself and proceeded with the prescribed devotion, giving it at least half his attention.

The angel of the Lord declared unto Mary
And she conceived by the Holy Ghost

(Good Lord, what a ridiculous thing to crop up from the past. One of his earliest priestly duties when he took over the parish had been to preside at the lavish wedding of the daughter of Frenchmen's Bay's richest citizen to a favored heir of the New Orleans aristocracy. He had not seen the couple or any of the family since the reception, at which he had gotten just a little tight.)

Holy Mary, Mother of God, pray for us sinners. . . .

(Coolly beautiful, the bride had been in *peau de soie* and French lace; the child would no doubt be homely. That's how it usually goes. He had heard of the woman's return to her mother's house; a parish priest is generally exposed to the more interesting items of local gossip. Middle-aged women in the confessional are more interested in discussing the sins of others than in owning up to their own. There had been much talk of multiple marriages and lip-smacking suggestions of alcoholism and promiscuity, but he had not been aware of the existence of a child.)

Behold the handmaid of the Lord,
Be it done unto me according to thy word. . . .

(He ought to have visited her, of course. His conscience was very bad on that score. He had a large parish, it was true, and he was kept busy enough with his faithful parishioners; yet it was his Master's command that he look after the lost sheep.)

Pray for us, holy Mother of God
That we may be made worthy of the promises of Christ. . . .

As the sound of the Angelus bell died away above him and the din of the convent dinner hour burst out behind him, he trotted up the rectory steps two at a time. It was Friday and there would be gumbo, dark and pungent with spices as mysterious as voodoo, rich with the meat of freshly caught crabs. Gumbo was another source of bad conscience, for its delights took all the sting out of the intended sacrifice of doing without flesh on Friday, turning an act of abstinence into a feast. But three hearty bowls of gumbo would put Monsignor Fulham in proper condition to withstand the onslaught of feigned tears and protestations of belated mother love that no doubt would greet his efforts to carry out Mother Ignatius' wishes. As he entered the rectory he took a deep breath, filling his lungs with the savor of gumbo.

3

MONSIGNOR FULHAM came to fetch the child early Saturday morning. He was asked to wait in the parlor, a large expensively furnished room which reminded him of a gallery in a museum, furnished for show rather than for use, with things that for all their individual beauty did not really go together. But at least it looked out on the bay. Monsignor Fulham turned his back on the room and stood before the large plate glass window, contemplating with awe how all the diversity of unrelated pieces of natural decoration somehow did go together. Between the house and the bay a quarter acre of green lawn stretched, disturbed only by an absurd marble Venus upon whose head a squirrel impudently perched, flicking its tail. Across Beach Drive, separated from it by a low seawall, the waters of Frenchmen's Bay lapped lackadaisically at the beach. A row of posts marched down the beach into the shallow water, the hurricane-spared remains of a pier. Pelicans resting between fishing trips sat upon the posts as still and self-confident as a row of military statues atop giant plinths. And the sun lay golden over everything.

Monsignor Fulham turned with a sigh back into the incongruous room. He heard footsteps approaching—high-heeled slippers. He turned toward the door, bracing himself for another tearful scene like the one yesterday. But as soon as the woman entered he knew that this interview would be different. This time he had been expected and she was ready for him, physically and emotionally. She had her makeup on and her bright blond hair neatly dressed. Monsignor Fulham, whose parishioners if they used makeup at all used it with blatant extravagance, had forgotten how effective a good paint job could be. His hostess had in each hand a tall glass filled with amber liquid, the ice cubes rattling invitingly with each movement. Monsignor Fulham did not hesitate to accept the glass offered him. Not that he was unaware that the woman he drank with was something of an alcoholic. He knew quite well that she had drunk before he came and she would drink after he left. But he also knew that his refusal to drink with her, while it could be taken as an insult, would do nothing to reform her habits.

They sat gingerly on fragile Louis XIV chairs. Monsignor Fulham looked around for somewhere to set his glass, but there was nothing close except a highly polished mahogany table. Finally he placed it on the Persian carpet next to his chair leg, reminding himself not to knock it over with his foot.

"These are the papers you wanted, I believe," the woman said, handing him two certificates. "I had the devil of a time finding them."

"Yes, thank you." Monsignor Fulham looked at the papers. One proclaimed the time, place and legitimacy of the birth of a white female and acknowledged her parentage. The second established that the infant had been duly baptized in the Catholic Church and had been given the name Guinevere Marie d'Arblay.

"Why Guinevere?" Monsignor Fulham asked half to himself. A short laugh came from the other Louis XIV chair.

"A private joke of sorts. Before she was born I was involved with a Lancelot of my own. My first husband's name was Arthur, and he thought the name was a compliment to him. I

15

guess he didn't know the story too well. When he did figure it out he sent me packing, baby and all. That's when I made my second mistake. I married my Lancelot."

She took a long drag at her drink, which she had not bothered to set down. Then she gave Monsignor Fulham a hard look.

"I told you yesterday that I had tried to be a good mother." She laughed again. It was not a pleasant laugh. "That is a slight exaggeration, in a manner of speaking. Actually I have done my level best to be no kind of mother at all. Some women are mothers and some women are just girls. I don't like being a mother so I'm giving the job up, for Guinevere's sake maybe but mostly for my own. You've given me a wonderful way out of at least some of my problems by offering to take her in. It's better for her and God knows it's better for me. I know the sisters will be nice to her, so I can feel free to forget about her myself. I want to get rid of my past and make a fresh start, you see. And she's part of my past. It's not her fault, but it's not mine either. So there it is."

With another gulp she emptied her glass. Monsignor Fulham managed with some effort to get his down to the halfway mark. He was less disturbed by this woman's admission than he might have been. He had too often sensed the same sentiments hidden behind the circumlocutions of too many "good mothers" in the confessional. That was one of the nice things about being rich, one could afford to be really honest.

The woman leaned forward with a sudden show of earnestness.

"You may think whatever you like about me, Father, but I won't have you teaching my girl that her mother's a wicked woman."

Monsignor Fulham half rose from his chair, his mouth opening to protest. She waved him down.

"I don't give a damn what else you teach her. You can make a little white virgin saint out of her as far as I'm concerned." She giggled. "She'd make a good saint, come to think of it. She's very good, really, just a little dumb, like her father."

16

She broke off quickly as the object of their discussion appeared in the doorway dressed in a highly inappropriate pink organza party dress and carrying her worldly goods in a green leather overnight bag. She wasn't, as Monsignor Fulham had feared, homely. She was reasonably pretty, though in no way striking; pale blond, rather than golden, a weak student copy of her mother.

"Send all bills to my bank," the mother muttered as she rose to give the child a farewell embrace. It was a painful gesture, unfamiliar and uncomfortable for both the giver and the receiver, ending with a maiden auntly kiss on the cheek.

"If you don't like it, sweetheart, you don't have to stay," the woman said without conviction.

"I'm sure I'll like it, Sylvia," the child replied in the same manner.

As they passed through the front door her mother repeated, "Send all bills to my bank."

It Was uncommonly quiet at the convent, for the boarding students spent their Saturday afternoons at the local movie house watching the inevitable Saturday double feature: a chaste Western followed by something comic or sentimental in black and white, with a serial adventure of the less horrific sort thrown in as a bonus.

Monsignor Fulham took the child up at once to meet Mother Ignatius. It was a quiet reception. The superior took her new student's hand in hers and smiled.

"I'm so pleased to have you here, my dear."

Guinevere did not answer her smile. Monsignor Fulham had noticed that. She never seemed to smile. Perhaps she hadn't learned how. She simply said, "Thank you," in a low, shy voice.

As the other boarders had not yet returned, Monsignor Fulham offered to show the child the church. He felt protective toward her and was not anxious just yet to release her into the alien life of the convent. He took her hand as they crossed the parking lot.

17

"I like her," the child said unexpectedly. "She has nice eyes."

"So she has," Monsignor Fulham replied, pleased. "And a very good heart to go with them."

"I'd like to talk to her," the child went on. "But I wasn't sure what I should call her. Some people get upset if you don't call them what they want."

"You should call her Mother," Monsignor Fulham explained.

"That's funny," Guinevere replied. "I'm supposed to call you Father and her Mother. I don't even call my own mother Mother. What do I call the others?"

"You call the other nuns Sister."

"That's funny, too. Is this the church? I don't think I've ever been in a church. Is it called anything but just church?"

"The church is called Star of the Sea."

"Oh." The child's eyes widened and she almost smiled. "I like that. It's very pretty."

Monsignor Fulham held the heavy west door open for her. Inside the church it was cool. The air was sweet with the odor of flowers and melting wax. It had a fairly decent fabric, the walls being white without too much gilding. The altar hangings and statuary were in fair taste for a provincial church, but the fresco that covered the domed ceiling above the high altar was a horror. The Immaculate Conception again, an empty-faced doll in garish blue surrounded by an aureole of painted gilt stars, pink and gold light beams streaming downward from her downstretched hands. Guinevere's eyes, like those of all people on first entering the church, strayed at once to the gaudy painting. She made a slight face and turned away.

"That's no Star of the Sea," she said in a scornful whisper.

"I quite agree with you." Monsignor Fulham was secretly pleased by her critical perception.

"But I like everything else," Guinevere added hastily, as though afraid of offending her new acquaintance by being critical of his property. "Especially all the little candles. They're pretty." She pointed to a row of flickering votives

18

like an oratorio choir on risers at the foot of a movingly simple unpainted wood statue of the Madonna and Child.

"Would you like to light a candle?" Monsignor Fulham asked.

"Oh, could I?" Guinevere managed somehow to look pleased without smiling.

Monsignor Fulham led her to the statue and, while helping her with the taper, surreptitiously slipped a nickel into the collection box. He felt uncomfortable about introducing this disturbingly guileless child to the financial side of his profession.

Guinevere stared, fascinated, into the tiny flame of her candle. "Do you make a wish, like a birthday?"

Monsignor Fulham suppressed a smile.

"Yes," he said. "You can tell her what you wish."

He watched her lips move silently, but could not read them.

SISTER CLEMENTINE was washing the statue in the Shrine, a chore which she described much to the chagrin of some of the more sensitive sisters as giving the Blessed Mother her Saturday bath. She stood on a stepladder in front of the nearly life-size statue with a bucket of hot suds dangling from the crook of her left arm, applying sponge and scrub brush diligently to the red clay, sand and bird droppings that clung to her Blessed Mother's plaster robe. She began to get the annoying feeling that she was being watched. It was to avoid an audience that she saved this particular job for Saturday afternoon, for it required her to tuck up the sleeves of her habit, exposing an immodest length of bony arm. She spun around quickly to see a single small blond girl in a silly-looking pink dress staring boldly at her. Sister Clementine stepped down from her perch, winding up for a good scolding. But she did not get to it. For as her movement exposed the statue to view, stunning in its shining cleanliness despite the trickle of soapsuds running down its cheeks like foamy tears, the child in the pink dress gave a cry of delight.

"Oh, it's her! It's her! Isn't she lovely?"

19

"Yes, she is," Sister Clementine had to admit, swallowing the hard words that had been rising to her lips. She could not scold anyone who so openly admired the object of all her labors. But she did manage to force some severity into her voice as she attempted to insure that all this enthusiasm would be tempered with proper respect.

"That is Our Blessed Mother."

The girl stood sturdily in front of the statue, studying it.

"That's the Star of the Sea," she affirmed confidently. "I know. You don't need to tell me. I wished to meet her and here she is. The Star of the Sea. It's nice to know she's a mother, too."

Sister Clementine was somewhat taken aback though she made no attempt to further clarify the identification, but proceeded to slosh the rest of the wash water over the base of the pedestal.

"I am Sister Clementine. I am the Custodian of Our Blessed Mother's Shrine."

"Hi. I'm Guinevere Simpson. I'm a new girl."

Without being asked and with easy disregard for the organza party dress she began helping Sister Clementine with her ablutions.

"I hate being a new girl in the middle of the year," she confided. "You never know what you're supposed to be doing. Is it all right for me to be here, Sister?"

"Certainly," said Sister Clementine. "You may come here any time you wish."

A noise not unlike the screaming of a flock of gulls came through the bushes. The boarders had returned from the show and had been let loose in the yard until suppertime. Sister Clementine rolled down her sleeves and picked up her sponge and scrub brush. Guinevere took the empty bucket and followed her up the path. She looked longingly back at the Shrine. Sister Clementine laid a gnarled hand on her shoulder.

"You may come to the Shrine any time you want, dear, and talk to Our Blessed Mother. She's a very good listener. She never interrupts."

She paused, waiting for her small companion to laugh. But she did not. She only nodded in agreement.

"That's very nice of her."

When they reached the source of the path Sister Clementine took the bucket and lumbered on her way back to the convent building. Guinevere stood for a few moments, painfully conspicuous in her fancy dress now decorated with gray splotches of dirty scrub water, watching the boarders in their blue uniforms playing at their own improvised version of the slapstick comedy they had just seen. There was no place in the game for a new girl who hadn't even seen the movie, and no effort was made to find a place for her. A few of the girls stopped long enough to stare curiously at her as they might at a strangely marked bird that had landed in their yard. They showed no open hostility but neither did they show friendliness. Guinevere sighed and pulled up a small yellow flower peering out of the dirt near her feet. It was such a nuisance being a new girl again, but it was better than lying in her room listening to Sylvia and Tony shout bad words at each other and waiting in dread for the crash of something falling.

She half turned as she felt something like a touch on her shoulder. But she saw nothing behind her except the path leading back to the little Shrine. Slowly she walked down between the stone borders, picking daisies and buttercups and those clusters of tiny yellow and pink flowers that the natives call hen-and-chicken. By the time she reached the green-roofed shelter she had collected a considerable bouquet. Standing directly in front of the coolly gazing statue, her feet in dusty patent leather dress shoes set wide apart, she addressed herself to the plaster figure.

"Hello," she said. "I picked these flowers. Do you want them?"

Slowly and gingerly she clambered up the pedestal and, holding tightly to the folds of the statue's blue mantle, reached to place the bunch of wilting flowers into the downstretched plaster hand.

21

4

It Was Monday morning and Sister Stephanie was trying to impose on the minds of her fifth graders the capitals of the states, not so much because this was important information to learn as because she felt such exercises to be as helpful in disciplining the recalcitrant mind as forced marches and cold showers in disciplining the body.

Jennie Freret squirmed uncomfortably at her desk, trying to concentrate on the collection of silly-looking names in front of her. New Jersey–Trenton, North Carolina–Raleigh, North Dakota–Bismarck. Now there was a name she'd have no trouble with. Her father used to own a horse named Bismarck. He hadn't been a very nice horse, but he had been a splendid jumper. He had broken his leg and had to be put down. Jennie made a quick line drawing of a horse in her notebook. If it were the other way around, she wondered, and horses owned men, would the horses kill people who broke their legs? Thinking about Bismarck depressed her. She modified her drawing so that the horse appeared to be relieving itself. That made her feel better somehow.

"Jennie!" Sister Stephanie's voice broke in sharply. "Are you with us, Jennie?"

"Yes, Sister." Jennie hastily covered the slightly scatological drawing in her notebook and scrambled to her feet.

"You have been paying attention, haven't you, Jennie?" Sister Stephanie prodded. The fifth grade giggled on cue in nervous relief, as one laughs at the fellow who slipped on the banana peel. "Since you have been so attentive I am sure you know what state I was just mentioning. Perhaps you can give me its capital."

"Yes, Sister," Jennie stammered. "The capital of—of North Dakota is Bismarck!"

The class gasped triumphant approval, and Jennie smiled to herself. This toss of the dice she had won, for a change.

"Very good, Jennie," Sister Stephanie said with a cool smile. "I am pleased to know that you are paying attention after all. You do a splendid imitation of daydreaming."

She had been building up for a long tirade on the evils of wandering minds when she deliberately called on Jennie and she wasn't about to waste it just because her example didn't turn out right. But fortunately for the class the recess bell rang before she had a chance to get well into it.

"Be sure you know all your capitals by tomorrow and have your maps ready for Friday."

Sister Stephanie rose and the class followed, mumbling in unison a hurried "Hail Mary," as rapid and careless as the closing of a book. All, that is, but Jennie Freret, who had been instructed by her pastor to take part in no prayer except the Lord's; and the new girl, who stood looking around confused, the way new girls do.

On the playground Jennie sought out the new girl. She must be a Protestant, too. Maybe they could be friends. Jennie wondered if the new girl liked horses. Probably not; she had a delicate, indoorsy look. She looked a little like a "brain," pale and solemn, but Jennie was sure she wasn't a "brain" because she read so badly. She spotted the new girl over near the washhouse. Tootsie Palmisano was talking to her. That was bad news. Jennie looked upon Tootsie as an enemy. Not only was she a Catholic, most of Jennie's friends were Catholics,

23

but she was a dago, one of those people who bred like rabbits (she had often heard her father say) and lived behind the railroad station, where the poor whites lived. The new girl would have to be rescued from such bad company.

"Hi"—she barged in, giving Tootsie a slight elbow in the ribs—"I'm Jennie Freret. I'm a non-Catholic. Are you?"

"I don't know, I'm new," the new girl said. "My name is Guinevere Simpson, and this is—uh—" She gestured uncertainly at Tootsie.

"I know her," Jennie snorted.

"Santuzza Palmisano, Tootsie for short," said Tootsie, returning the dig in the ribs with interest. "It's a funny name, isn't it?"

"Hysterical," Jennie muttered, bumping Tootsie with her hip. She didn't know exactly what the word meant, but it was the sort of thing her mother said when she wanted to be sarcastic.

"It's from opera," Tootsie went on, giving one of Jennie's long braids a surreptitious yank. "We all have opera names. Papa loves the opera almost as much as he loves kids. Ow! You get your filthy Protestant shoe off my toe, Jennie Freret, or I'll tell Sister."

The new girl gave Jennie a strange look and she retreated.

"Sorry, Toots. It was an accident."

The pause gave her a chance to turn the conversation away from Tootsie.

"I didn't know your name was Simpson. I thought Sister said something else, something French." Jennie's grandfather was French. That should give her some advantage over Tootsie, who was dago through and through.

"D'Arblay," the new girl said. "That's my first father's name."

"How many fathers have you got?" asked Jennie, impressed.

Guinevere thought a moment. "Three."

"Gee," Tootsie gasped. She had to share one father amongst nine kids. She couldn't imagine the delight of having even one father to herself. "You-all must have a ball at your place."

24

Guinevere shook her head. "They're not much fun. They just yell at you to shut up because they have a hangover. Anyhow, I don't have them all at once. They come and go. Like boyfriends, but different. They are different, fathers and boyfriends, have you noticed?"

She stopped suddenly, as though startled by her own effusiveness. Her two companions stared at her in openmouthed silence.

"It took me a while to figure it out," Guinevere continued a little uncertainly. "It's the rings that do it. Fathers give rings and boyfriends give other stuff. I don't know what's so great about a plain old ring. The stuff the boyfriends give is much prettier, necklaces and big sparkly pins, stuff like that. It does make a difference, though. When fathers leave there's always more of a fuss, and they take the rings back. The boyfriends mostly don't take their stuff back. But Mother Ignatius says only the first father really counts; the others are all just boyfriends, ring or no ring. I don't get it. It's all kind of silly, I think. Most grown-up stuff is silly."

On that the other girls could readily agree. Tootsie pushed her long black ringlets back from her face.

"Gee," she said. "We've only got one papa, one mama and nine kids. No boyfriends at all. And nobody never leaves."

"I wish I could change fathers sometimes," Jennie murmured. She gave the new girl a brilliant smile. "Let's be friends, OK?"

"OK," Guinevere said, naïvely including Tootsie in the invitation. "We'll all be friends." She joined the two rivals in a symbolic embrace. Jennie squirmed free, grimacing.

"Hey, I've got to be excused," Tootsie cried hastily, preventing Jennie from voicing her objections. "You-all come with me."

Jennie shrugged and assented. Guinevere followed them down to the small lavatory on the far side of the washhouse. She wasn't certain what being excused meant, but as a frequent new girl she knew that it was best not to ask, only to observe.

25

The three girls were excused together in adjoining doorless cubicles. The act of passing simultaneous water in fellowship had the effect of binding their newfound friendship and ironing over differences which really did not belong to them. Grown-up fears and prejudices don't have a chance in the camaraderie of the toilet.

Summoned back by the bell warning of the approaching end of recess, the girls once more passed the washhouse. Sister Lucy stood in the doorway wiping her reddened hands on her apron. She smiled broadly at the trio.

"Good morning, good morning," she called in a light-voiced singsong, bobbing up and down like the Chinese servant in a comedy.

"Good morning, Sister," they murmured, nervously hurrying past.

"That's Sister Lucy," Jennie whispered. "She's kind of batty."

"Papa says she ain't," Tootsie interposed. "He says she acts funny because she's retarded."

"What's retarded?" Jennie asked.

"I'm not sure, but it ain't the same as batty. I think it's sort of like being a little kid except you're a grown-up. Papa says she's real nice."

"She looks kind of nice," said Guinevere. "I don't care if people are a little funny in the head, just so they're nice."

"Dumb people are nice, mostly," said Tootsie.

"Yeah, it's the brains that're so darned snooty," Jennie agreed.

The three friends marched into the fifth grade classroom with their arms firmly linked, announcing publicly a new alliance which the rest would have to honor. During the remainder of the morning they confirmed the bond by passing one another silly notes.

At Three o'clock each afternoon (three-thirty for the high school) classes were dismissed, and for the day students at least school was over. A few tarried in the yard for one reason or another, but after four o'clock, with few exceptions, the convent, building and grounds, belonged to the boarders, that motley but exclusive minority that lived together there like a cumbersome extended family. And from the close of classes until supper at six they were as free as boarders in a convent school ever are.

Marianne Brandon, senior boarder and proctor of Dormitory B, settled herself on one of the green park benches beside the stone-lined path with a novel she was reading. She had borrowed it from the high school library in the belief that it was a light romance of the sort favored by high school girls. She had not gotten very far into it before she realized that it was quite another sort of book—certainly not the sort of book that ought to be in a convent library. Marianne knew that her duty was to inform Sister Anne-Marie, who served as librarian, of the true nature of the book contaminating her chaste shelves. But until she saw Sister Anne-Marie, whom she had been doing her best to avoid, she figured she might as well continue reading the scandalous tale to make certain that she had judged it correctly.

She looked up furtively from her reading as a black habit intruded on her line of vision. No, it wasn't Sister Anne-Marie, just old Sister Clementine in gray apron and garden gloves. Walking just behind her was the new girl. Marianne wondered why the new girl hung around the Shrine so much instead of playing with the others. Since the new girl was in her dormitory Marianne felt some responsibility for her. She closed the novel, which she had carefully camouflaged in a paper textbook cover advertising a local market, and walked over to the girl.

"Hot, isn't it?"

The new girl smiled diffidently, pleased at being noticed by a senior. "It's cooler down at the Shrine."

Marianne made another attack. "Are you getting along OK? Do you like it here?"

"Sure," the new girl said. "It's all right. You get lots to eat."

Marianne pointed to a group of younger boarders busy

27

playing a variation of hopscotch which involved in some way guessing the names of movie stars.

"Don't you want to play?" she asked.

Guinevere shook her head.

"I'm no good at it. I don't know very many movie stars and I get mixed up. I can't tell the difference between Lucille Ball and Arlene Dahl." She giggled, then turned away with a shrug. "Anyhow, they don't want me."

So that's it, Marianne thought. The Treatment. As most of her growing years had been spent in boarding schools she was familiar with the Treatment, the systematic ostracism of any-one who dared to defy the binding rules of the community of boarding students.

"What's the trouble?" she asked.

Guinevere sighed. "Oh, I don't know, I'm just all wrong. I'm a new girl and I don't know the right way to do things. I eat bacon with my fingers and don't know the 'Hail Mary.' I have lace on my underwear and short pants on my pajamas. And I fold my napkin wrong. But I don't care. I've got my own friends. Real good friends. Tootsie Palmisano and Jennie Freret are my very best friends. We've sworn."

Marianne groaned inwardly. So that was it. She had broken one of the most sacred taboos of convent society. She had married outside the tribe. For, although casual acquaintance was permitted, no boarder ever developed a close bond of friendship with a day student. Marianne wondered if she ought to explain the situation to the new girl. She'd have to think about that.

"Oh well," she said, putting her arm around Guinevere's shoulders. "Don't you mind the others. I'm your friend, too. Come on, let's go be excused before lunch."

"OK," said Guinevere, proud to be sharing the ritual of elimination with so eminent a boarder. She looked pointedly at the group playing hopscotch.

They went to the rest room in the convent basement re-served for high school girls during class hours but open to all boarders at other times. It had doors on every booth. At the present time it was filled with Latin American girls of all ages gaggling rapid Spanish at one another. Perhaps a third of the boarding population at Holy Innocents consisted of the daughters of well-to-do landowners in the banana republics of Central America and the Caribbean who had been sent north into the care of the nuns to prepare for entry into the better colleges or to escape recurring revolutions, or both. They formed an exclusive community within the exclusive community of the convent, in it but not of it.

Lunch, so termed, it almost seemed, to confuse new girls, occurred between dinner (noon) and supper (evening), and consisted of milk and cookies or something similar. The hopscotch group sat at one long table in the basement lounge as far distant as possible from the new girl and her protector. The dark-eyed Latins sat together near the pair, for the barrier of language made spatial distance irrelevant.

"I have another friend, too," Guinevere chattered between sips of cold milk. "She's the best of all. She told me not to bother with them." She indicated the hopscotchers. "She says their souls are too small. She likes Jennie and Tootsie, though, and you, too. But Sister Clementine doesn't think I should tell anybody about her. She says most people wouldn't understand. I don't know what she means by that, but I'm a new girl, so there's lots I don't know."

Marianne could not make much sense of this jumbled speech. But before she could ask Guinevere just what she was talking about, she was forced by a pointed cough directly above her to look up. Sister Anne-Marie stood smiling down upon her.

"Excuse me, Marianne, but I believe you have a book overdue from the library."

Marianne made a guilty grab for the covered book.

"It's—it's not overdue, Sister," she stammered. It wasn't. She had had it only four days. But apparently its true nature had come to light. Sister Anne-Marie said nothing but continued to hold out her hand.

Blushing, Marianne surrendered the improper book. After

29

nine years with the nuns she still didn't know how they did it. Perhaps they really did work under divine inspiration. In any event, it was a proven fact that no student, not even a senior dorm proctor, could get the best of them.

5

ONLY HALF of the proud new brick annex was used for elementary classrooms. The other half, that farthest from the convent, housed a large gymnasium-cum-auditorium, equipped primarily for use as a basketball court, but admirably adaptable to other purposes. On the too shallow, too wide stage at one end of the gym, better designed for assemblies and graduations than for theatrics, Sister Helen through April and most of May somewhat desperately was rehearsing the principals for the spring show. In honor of the new building as well as in an effort to pay for it, she had decided to launch a full-blown musical, *The Wizard of Oz*. It was an ambitious project, one which Sister Helen soon began to regret somewhat. Not that she didn't have all the help she could use: the senior art classes were making sets, brightly painted and delicately fantastic; the home ec girls designed and constructed showy costumes of nylon and chintz; and those students capable of playing a musical instrument reasonably well had gotten together to form a passable combo. But there were other, less obvious problems. The casting, for one thing, bothered Sister Helen. She intensely disliked having to make choices of that sort, choices that were seldom really satisfactory—artistic and political compromises. If art had been the only consideration (what impresario has ever worked in the paradise where that is the case?), she would simply have filled the cast with all available Palmisanos. This she had not been permitted to do. Mother Ignatius had made it plain to her from the start, in her gentle, subtle way, that the purpose of the show was to raise money. The leading roles, especially that of Dorothy, ought to be given to talented girls, of course, but if at all possible to talented girls with wealthy and generous parents. Sister Helen was neither shocked nor incensed by this suggestion, but she was a little disappointed at having to abandon her plan of giving the lead to Tootsie Palmisano. It went instead to Tootsie's now inseparable companion, Jennie Freret, who could hope to draw in townspeople, even Protestants, who, since they took advantage of the superior education the convent provided their daughters, ought to do their share in keeping it in good running order. Jennie's voice was not wholly satisfactory, although she managed to stay on pitch most of the time, but at least she looked the part and, having been brought up among horses, was easy to train.

Most of the rehearsals for the leading parts were held after school, and when Jennie was practicing, which was almost every spring afternoon, her two best friends, the rejected Tootsie and that new child, whose name Sister Helen could not remember, sat together on a bench on the side of the basketball court. Tootsie often did her homework, but the other child always watched, sitting quite still, her arms wrapped about her knees, her mouth open, her rather pallid blue eyes staring fixedly at the stage.

There was only a week of rehearsal left, and Sister Helen was in quiet despair. Everything appeared to be going well, technically, but she knew there was no real life in it. Sister Helen bit her lip nervously as she watched Jennie and the three high school girls who played the Scarecrow, the Tin Man and the Lion ploddingly struggling to conquer the mime walk. Five-year-old Figaro, the only Palmisano who had managed to make the cast, cavorted on all fours behind them. He

32

was playing Toto, Dorothy's dog, unfortunately a nonsinging part. However, even on all fours he was the only one who could do a convincing mime walk.

"Oh, for heaven's sake," Sister Helen wailed, suddenly swinging herself over the stage apron with surprising agility for her age and corpulence. "You-all are dead, walking like zombies. This isn't the Saturday double feature. And that road isn't Railroad Avenue on Sunday morning. It's the Yellow Brick Road, the one and only original Yellow Brick Road leading straight into the land of your heart's desire." Her voice rose, sharp and resonant with excitement. "Follow it! There it is! Can't you see it, at your very feet, shining in the sun like burnished gold, beckoning you on?" She pointed dramatically at the scuffed wood stage floor. "Look at it! See it! Follow it!"

"I don't see anything, Sister," Jennie protested, staring down at the row of floorboards.

The older girls snickered, and Sister Helen clutched at her veiled head. "Well, Jennie, if you can't see it at least you can feel it. Like this. Watch me now."

She tucked up the many skirts of her habit and sang as she strutted in place.

"Follow the Yellow Brick Road,
Follow the Yellow Brick Road,
Follow, follow, follow, follow
Follow the Yellow Brick Road. . . ."

The two girls watching began to giggle. It was a ludicrous sight: Sister Helen, plump and dignified, playing the clown in thick black stockings and high-topped oxfords. The laughter spread, first to Marianne Brandon, who was serving as rehearsal pianist, then to the actors on stage. Sister Helen stopped abruptly, spun around and glowered at them all. Some faces are made to show a scowl to good advantage and can with a look intimidate the boldest. It was with such a face that Sister Helen had been blessed. Her scowl struck the girls like a thunderbolt. They swallowed their mirth in one collective

33

guilty gulp and tried to concentrate on the mime walk. They were all afraid of Sister Helen, not with the tender awe they felt for Mother Ignatius, but with a positive, resenting fear. They had no way of knowing, young as they were and imprisoned by their fear of the power and authority that seemed forever surrounding them, that behind her mask of indignation Sister Helen was laughing as well.

"All right, girls," she said after a disturbingly long silence. "I think that will do for now. Practice the mime walk at home in front of a mirror, heel-toe, heel-toe, and we'll try again tomorrow." She paused, glaring pointedly at the two little girls cowering on the bench. "Without an audience!"

"Oh, please, Sister, please. We'll be quiet, really we will. Please let us come."

Sister Helen looked at the two children pleading tearfully to her. She disliked tears and pleading. They made her painfully aware of her ability to cause unhappiness in those under her authority.

"I can't afford interruptions like this. . . ."

"It won't happen again, Sister, really it won't. Please give us a chance."

"Very well," Sister Helen said with a show of reluctance. "But if I hear another sound from you . . ."

"Oh, thank you, Sister. Thank you."

Jennie hopped down from the stage into the arms of her friends, and the three skipped out of the gym arm in arm, singing loudly their victory. Figaro trotted, ignored, a few feet behind.

Jennie's mother was waiting for her in the school yard in a large, well-used station wagon. She reached over to open the right-hand door.

"Hurry, dear. I have to stop at the market."

"OK, Mom. I'm coming," Jennie called. "Can we give Tootsie a lift?"

Jennie's mother frowned slightly. "Well, dear, we really do have to shop and it's a bit out of our way. . . ."

"That's OK, Jen," Tootsie said quickly. "I've got my bike."

34

"No, you don't," Figaro objected shrilly. Amongst the nine young Palmisanos there was not even one bicycle.

"Shut up," Tootsie snapped. "See you tomorrow, Jennie."

The large station wagon backed out of the school yard and sped away along Beach Drive. Tootsie and Guinevere walked down the path leading to the Shrine, turning off just at the grove of trees and crossing to a small dirt road that led from the back of the convent grounds toward the inland section of town. Figaro followed, dragging his feet and kicking up dust.

Tootsie giggled. "Jennie's mother looks a lot like a horse, don't she?"

"I guess that's because she's around horses so much," said Guinevere. "I hope Jennie doesn't grow up to look like a horse."

"My papa says people grow to look like the things they love. He says that's why Mama looks like a dish of spaghetti."

"What does your mama say then?" Guinevere was always eager to hear details of Palmisano family life.

"Oh, she says she won't give him no supper. But she always does. They joke around a lot like that."

The girls stood leaning on the posts of the broken gate that opened onto the back road. A pair of iridescent green dragonflies, named by the grateful natives "mosquito hawks," darted at each other amorously.

"Did you see it?" Guinevere asked suddenly.

Tootsie spun around, searching the vicinity for what she might be expected to see. "What? The mosquito hawks?"

"No, dummy. The Yellow Brick Road."

"Oh." Tootsie thought for a moment. "Yeah, I guess I did, sort of. When Sister Helen was jumping around and pointing and all, I thought I saw it, just for a second. It looked kind of like that road that goes through St. Joseph's Cemetery on All Saints' Day, when the graves are all decorated with flowers and stuff. It ain't yellow brick, but it's the prettiest road I ever seen." She drew lines in the dirt with the worn toe of her oxford. "I wonder if there really is such a thing as yellow bricks. I never seen any. Did you see it?"

Guinevere shook her head. "No, I didn't see it, but it's got to be there if Sister Helen saw it. I don't think I was looking right. Maybe you can only see it when you get all worked up and jump around like Sister Helen did. Maybe you should try that tomorrow."

"Yeah," Tootsie mused. "Maybe it would work for me."

With a triumphant whoop Figaro pulled from the pile of earth he had disturbed with his stub of stick a single parched earthworm. This he dangled impudently in front of his sister's nose. Guinevere recoiled, but Tootsie, who had endured three elder brothers and one younger, took the squirming prey from him and gently replanted it in a shady moist spot.

"You ought to see yourself, Figgy," she scolded, grabbing him by the arm and shaking him. "You're just filthy. Whatever will Mama say? I hope she spanks you, brat! Hey, I better go, Gwen. It's getting late and Papa's on night duty again. I'll see you tomorrow."

"So long, Toots," Guinevere called after her as she started down the road dragging the whimpering Figaro.

Guinevere walked slowly back toward the convent. She turned at the path leading down through the grove of trees to the Shrine. It certainly didn't look like yellow brick. Suddenly she spun around as if tapped on the shoulder. Two girls from her dorm and from her table stood together by the ball court watching her. They looked away when their eyes caught hers. But they did not move. Sighing, Guinevere returned up the path to the yard and mounted the deserted merry-go-round, sending it slowly spinning with a single strong push of her foot. The two girls from her dorm and her table walked by arm in arm, carefully looking the other way.

"Do you ever play on the merry-go-round, Judy?" one asked the other loudly.

"Course not, silly," Judy replied, sharp with scorn. "The merry-go-round's for babies."

They turned back and headed for the convent, giggling and occasionally whispering the word "baby" amidst loud bursts of laughter. Guinevere gave the merry-go-round a vicious push, causing it to spin around rapidly. Then she jumped off while it was going full speed and trudged slowly across the dusk-silent gray playground to the convent and the dubious bounty of lunch.

THAT NIGHT was a clear one, bright with the unshaded light of a near full moon. The air was still and heavy with early summer moisture. The convent lay in silence and darkness. Everyone, even Mother Ignatius, had gone to bed. The students' narrow cots were arranged in rows down the lengths of the large, high-ceilinged dormitory rooms, against the windowless side walls and head to head along the center. Each bed as well as the small metal dresser that went with it was surrounded by a screen of white curtain, like the beds in a hospital ward. A nun slept in a curtained alcove at each corner of each dorm like the four angels in a child's bedside prayer. Only the red sanctuary lamp and the shaded votive lights in the nuns' chapel remained on, indicating that there was still one sleepless eye watching over all that white-curtained chastity.

Marianne Brandon sat on a straight chair by the large open window at the far end of Dormitory B, breathing the heady scent of the magnolias blooming just outside the window and listening to the halfhearted slap of the bay against the beach. Someone in the curtained dorm was snoring. Marianne lay her head on the cool dark wood windowsill, trying to still her overactive mind.

That evening the seniors had brought out their prom gowns for inspection by Sister Helen, who, as arbiter of virgin modesty, had to pass on the amount of uncovered flesh permitted in the presence of young males. Marianne's, of course, had passed inspection easily, for it was not, like so many of them, one of the popular strapless gowns temporarily made acceptable by a bit of cape or a lacy bolero. Hers was made with sleeves and a convent-proper neckline. Her mother had cleverly copied the portrait of a Victorian great-aunt, giving a feeling of authenticity to the enforced modesty of the gown.

37

That was a typical strategy of Marianne's mother. She was well blessed with the southern woman's talent for always getting her own way while appearing to live only for the joy of pleasing others. And she was in her own quiet way almost impossible to cross. Marianne had made one more attempt at it during Easter vacation. She had gone home filled with the firmest of resolves. Time was getting short, she would be graduating in two months, and after hearing endless speeches on the commencement of her adulthood, she would supposedly find herself free to follow the life of her choice. Marianne laughed to herself at that, for she was beginning to realize as she approached that goal she had worked toward so hard the last four years how carefully the way had been laid for her already, how little real choice she had. The raucous whistle of the 10:07, the gleaming silver Crescent Limited on its way up the East Coast from New Orleans to Boston by way of Atlanta, Washington, New York, howled in the distance. Now there was a choice, if she dared make it. She wondered what would happen if she just hopped down from the gym stage in her white cap and gown clutching her ribboned diploma, waved them all good-bye and went off on the 10:07 for—wherever it took her. She laughed again, this time at herself, for she knew she hadn't the courage for such an ambitious commencement. Why, she hadn't even the courage to tell her mother that she wasn't going to that nice private college where she could meet nice young men, having a lovely wedding with her picture on the front of the Sunday society page of the *Times-Picayune*, and settling down in someplace like Mobile to raise beautiful children (not too many) and play bridge. What a bore.

The subject of her future plans came up while her mother was giving the green tulle and brocade prom gown a final fitting. She had put off too long, her mother scolded, applying to one of the better colleges and would have little chance of getting in now. Marianne had not let on that she had put the matter off on purpose. Would it perhaps be wisest after all, her mother had suggested, to take a year or so off and get a foothold in local society before she went away again?

"Mother Ignatius can get me into Ursuline this fall," Marianne had interposed quickly, terrified by the threat of local society.

"Oh no," her mother had countered. "Not another girls' school. That's all right, my dear, for little girls, but now . . ." Her voice had trailed off loud with things unsaid. Then she muttered through the pins in her mouth, "You may as well enter the convent and be done with it."

There it had been, the moment she had been waiting for, with the subject brought up by someone else. But she let the moment pass, knowing that a better one would not come along. And the matter was left at that, to be explored in some indefinite future time when all the excitement of prom and parties and graduation had cooled down. Marianne, cursing her cowardice, had given in to her mother as usual and kept her vocation to herself.

Now that she had been back at the convent for a few weeks, she was beginning to wonder if it might not have been her guardian angel rather than her cowardice that had stayed her tongue. For now as she listened to the 10:07 whistle and clack into the distance, she was beginning to question that vocation all the sisters were sure she had. Wasn't she being railroaded into the religious life here as surely as she was being shoved into her proper place in society at home? She had never herself so much as expressed a desire to enter the convent, not in so many words, not that she could remember, anyway. It was simply taken for granted; she was so good with the younger children, so serious and reliable. Her date for the prom was himself known to be a candidate for seminary. Why of all the available girls at the convent had the sisters recommended him to her? Because they were both "safe" for each other. And why, in heaven's name, had she meekly acquiesced and asked him? What a bore. What a miserable bore. It might have been fun, like a last fling, to have asked someone exciting and have had one real date. Oh well, no one interesting would have accepted. It was better, she supposed, if one must be an old maid, to be one by choice and not just a marital leftover pouring endless cups of coffee at church receptions.

Outside a silly night bird was chirping hysterically for its mate. The whistle of the 10:07 died away in the distance. Marianne turned from the window. It was nearly eleven; she ought to try to get to sleep. She'd say the Rosary; that often helped when she was restless, soothing her into rest with its pious monotony. Pausing with her hands on her drawn bed curtains, she glanced at the bed whose head lay against hers. Guinevere d'Arblay, the poor new little girl who was being so ruthlessly subjected to the Treatment by her contemporaries. Marianne was only too familiar with the Treatment. She had felt its sting and bore its scars. So she made a point of paying special attention to Guinevere and had sat on the edge of her bed talking to her every night since she had come to the convent. Tonight, distracted by her own musings, she had forgotten. Marianne wondered if the girl might possibly still be awake. Cautiously she drew back the curtains around the child's bed. The covers had been thrown back and the bed was empty.

Marianne sat down hard on the empty bed, reminding herself not to panic. What ought she to do? Waken Sister Stephanie, who guarded the nearest corner, and raise the alarm? No, wait. Perhaps the child had only gone down the hall to excuse herself. Quickly Marianne pulled on her robe and ran down the silent corridor, trying to keep her backless scuffs from clattering on the linoleum. The lavatory was terribly empty and silent except for a single faucet dripping a lonely tattoo in the middle of a row of silent washbasins. Marianne pivoted on one toe, scurried the length of the dim corridor and down the main staircase.

The second floor lay in unnatural quiet, like a recently haunted house. A noise, a scratching sound, then a rasping squeak, came from the seventh grade classroom. Clinging to the wall, her heart beating audibly, Marianne forced herself to go to the door of the room. A small figure in lace-trimmed short pajamas was climbing in a window from the veranda. She closed the window behind her with another squeak and a soft click.

"Guinevere!" Marianne cried in a shrill whisper.

The girl spun around, backing up against the window as if poised for flight, staring in terror at the darkness in front of her.

"Who is it? Who's there?"

"Marianne Brandon. Come here at once."

Relief turning at once to irrational rage, Marianne seized the approaching child by the shoulders and began shaking her violently.

"What do you think you're doing, sneaking out like that?" she gasped. "What are you up to, anyway, you little devil? Trying to get me in trouble? Judas Priest, you gave me a scare!"

Guinevere began sobbing loudly, going limp in Marianne's arms. The older girl quickly pulled her into the chapel, closing the door behind her, sat down with her in a front pew and wrapped her in a comforting embrace. Anger dissolved into tenderness.

"All right, punkin, don't cry. I'm sorry. I was frightened, that's all." Groping in the deep pockets of her robe, she extracted a decaying Kleenex, which she gave to Guinevere.

"I'm sorry, Marianne. I didn't mean to frighten you," Guinevere whimpered, cuddling in Marianne's arms.

"It's against rules to go out at night," Marianne said gently. "You could get us both in awful trouble if the sisters found out. Besides, it could be dangerous."

Guinevere shook her head. "Not for me. I'm protected. She told me I would come to no harm. That's exactly what she said. But I won't go at night anymore if it worries you." She sighed. "It's just so much better at night when nobody's around."

"Good God," cried Marianne. "Have you been out there

41

before?" She tried to disguise the fear that was rising in her throat and kept the questioning as gentle and relaxed as possible. "Are you meeting someone, punkin?"

Guinevere nodded. "Sister Clementine told me not to talk about her. I've only told Tootsie and Jennie because they're best friends. It's not allowed to keep secrets from best friends."

Marianne pulled a long face. "I thought I was your friend, too."

"Oh, you are, you are." Guinevere smiled suddenly. "Then it would be OK to tell you, too, wouldn't it?"

"Oh yes. I'm sure it's OK to tell me."

Marianne felt only triumph at the success of her little trick. There would be time enough to feel guilt about it later.

The red sanctuary lamp twinkled unsteadily, causing the statues to cast weird shadows on the walls. The little red votive light at the foot of the Infant of Prague sputtered and went out. Guinevere rose slowly, genuflected and crossed the chapel to the Immaculate Conception, enthroned in a niche in the far wall. She touched the globe at the base of the image affectionately and smiled up into the statue's insipid face, the row of candles below lighting her own face like an aureole and giving her rather nondescript features a beauty they did not naturally possess. She turned to Marianne, who had remained seated, stunned, in the pew.

"It's her, Marianne. It's her. The Star of the Sea. She lives at the Shrine. I go there all the time to visit her. She's my very, very best friend."

6

AT PRECISELY seven-thirty in the morning bells rang throughout the convent, rousing the boarders from their curtained sleep. At precisely seven forty-five the bells rang again, and the boarders, vaguely awake and dressed all alike in dark blue skirts and light blue blouses, lined up two by two in order of seniority at the head of the main staircase. In silence they marched behind Sister Stephanie and in front of Sister Anne-Marie down the stairs to the refectory. Sister Helen walked alongside in the manner of a drill sergeant, keeping an eye out for the odd nudge or surreptitious whisper.

The refectory tables were round and seated eight, usually girls from the same grade or at least from the same dorm. At each place was an orange neatly cut in eighths. After asking God's blessing on the oranges and all that would follow them, the girls consumed them in silence while Sister Anne-Marie read from the *Lives of the Saints*. That day she read of St. Dorothea, who lived alone in a tiny cell with only visions of God and the saints to keep her company. Marianne Brandon squirmed uneasily, for she found all this talk of heavenly visitations very disconcerting. She shot a quick look at the middle elementary table, where Guinevere d'Arblay sat listening raptly, sucking on an orange segment. Marianne bit her lip. She wished to heaven she hadn't asked the questions she had last night; the knowledge she had gained now weighed on her like a burden too heavy for her to carry. And she did not know what to do with it.

When the reading was over the girls rose one table at a time in order of seniority and took their plates of orange peel to the cafeteria-like counter at the end of the refectory. In return for this dish each received a large dinner plate containing a lump of scrambled egg, one dryly overdone sausage pattie and a generous helping of grits, that inevitable paste-white starchy southern breakfast food, decorated with a single pat of butter.

Once the girls had returned to their seats they were permitted a little subdued conversation. Sister Lucy passed amongst the tables bearing a tray on which were a number of large pitchers filled with coffee blended with hot milk in the French manner. Each table had its own pitcher, but when no nun was looking, Brenda Sue Foote slipped over to a senior table and filled her cup from the senior pitcher. For everyone knew that the contents of the pitchers corresponded in ratio of milk to coffee according to the seniority of the students drinking it, and Brenda Sue liked her coffee strong.

Although the youngest girl at her table, Brenda Sue seemed the most mature and therefore was the unchallenged leader. Brenda Sue and her four older sisters spent the school year at the convent, but during the summer months managed on their own at a coastal cottage, where their parents, who lived and worked in New Orleans, visited them on occasional weekends. Their free, almost unsupervised, existence had given them a veneer of sophistication that demanded the envious respect of the other students. Conversation at the middle elementary table was dominated by Brenda Sue as she charmed and annoyed her compatriots with tales of long summer afternoons in which the Foote girls whiled away the time giving one another home permanents and reading love story magazines. Only those in Brenda Sue's favor were allowed to participate in the conversation, so Guinevere d'Arblay ate, as always, in

44

silence. But she didn't seem to mind, nor did she seem to take any interest in the talk around her. She concentrated on the contents of her plate, disposing of them with the desperate single-mindedness of the man who doesn't know where his next meal is coming from.

Brenda Sue turned with a sourly amused look and the table lapsed into disapproving silence as all observed her scooping up the last morsels of grits onto her coffee spoon with the assistance of one stubby forefinger.

"Hey, kid," said Brenda Sue in her startlingly deep voice, "were you brought up in the barnyard with the little piggies?"

Everyone laughed. Guinevere sucked apologetically on her forefinger.

"It's all so good I hate to waste any."

"Want mine, kid?" Brenda Sue indicated her own pile of grits, rejected out of hand as lumpy and fattening.

Guinevere nodded eagerly, scraping the proffered grits onto her plate. "Gee, thanks, Brenda Sue."

The other girls mercilessly watched her eat.

"My God, I think she'd eat fried manure," Brenda Sue remarked in a stage whisper.

Guinevere blushed, but continued eating the grits. When only a morsel remained at the side of the plate she looked up and gave Brenda Sue a long defiant stare. She then scooped up the morsel onto her coffee spoon with her forefinger, which she licked clean. She looked steadily at them all, and no one laughed.

After Breakfast Sister Anne-Marie opened the library for the use of the few "brains" who seemed practically to live there and the infrequent senior struggling with an overdue term paper. Her only client this morning was Marianne Brandon, looking somewhat distracted. She took from the shelf a copy of the *Lives of the Saints* and began thumbing through it. Sister Anne-Marie came over to her, wondering if she could be of some help.

Marianne looked up.

45

"Do you believe all this, Sister? I mean like you were read-ing about at breakfast. Our Lord and the saints appearing to people. Do you believe that? I mean really believe it?"

Sister Anne-Marie smiled sympathetically at this manifes-tation of honest doubt.

"As a faithful daughter of the Church I believe all such things that the Church has judged to be true visions and not works of the devil. That is all that is required of us."

Marianne scowled. "Yes, Sister. I know that, but it still doesn't answer my question. I mean do you *really* believe it? In your heart?"

Sister Anne-Marie spluttered a little. "I really believe every-thing the Church requires me to believe. Don't you?"

"Oh yes, sure." Marianne turned back to the book, biting her nails, and Sister Anne-Marie once more occupied herself with updating the card catalogue.

"Like this!" Marianne exclaimed suddenly. She read from the text before her. " 'Saint Daniel the Stylite was ordained to the priesthood while he stood on a balustrade atop a twelve-foot-high pillar near Constantinople. He remained there for thirty-three years without ever sitting or lying down. People came from everywhere to see him and to hear him preach, and kings and emperors sought his counsel.' Really, Sister, doesn't that seem a bit much to swallow? And you remember St. Lucy. You read about her last winter. The Romans con-demned her to a house of ill-fame, but they couldn't move her. She was stuck to the floor. Even a yoke of oxen couldn't budge her. They finally had to light a fire under her right in the courtroom."

"The fire would not burn her," Sister Anne-Marie recalled. "Finally a soldier had to pierce her heart with a sword. I do not think we are required to believe every detail of such sto-ries provided we do believe that miracles of God have oc-curred and that many saints have been blessed with wondrous visions."

"Yeah," Marianne said. "I see what you mean. But—but just suppose it wasn't something in a book that happened a long time ago. Suppose right now somebody you knew told you she had seen a vision, somebody you were sure wouldn't lie, but the Church didn't know about it or anything, what would you do?"

Sister Anne-Marie smiled. Here she was on familiar ground. A typical schoolgirl "what-if," the sort she dealt with daily in her seventh grade religion classes. Years of training and experience as well as the memory of all such questions she had asked in her own skeptical youth had supplied her with answers as ready and automatic as those in the Catechism.

"I should take the information at once to some trustworthy person in authority, preferably a priest. It is unwise for a layman to attempt to deal with such matters on his own."

She slammed the drawer of the card catalogue with a firm snap and stood at the open library door, waiting with a show of patience for Marianne to return the *Lives of the Saints* to its shelf. The first bell rang to warn of the imminent start of the school day.

"That's easier said than done," Marianne muttered.

"Anyway," Sister Anne-Marie concluded cheerily, "I don't think it's a problem we really have to concern ourselves with, is it? A sleepy little convent is hardly a prime target for miracles and heavenly visitations."

"That's what I would have thought." Marianne's voice began to rise. "But . . ."

"But what?" Sister Anne-Marie raised her eyes suddenly and looked straight at Marianne. "Just what are you driving at?"

And Marianne told her, quickly, bluntly, feeling free to transfer her burden, having been assured that it was her duty to pass it on to shoulders of greater wisdom and authority.

Sister Anne-Marie took up the burden easily, as she did most things, without bothering to measure or weigh it. It seemed at first glance so easy and familiar, the sort of thing that cropped up regularly in religious communities. And she had a prescribed answer ready at hand.

"I shouldn't concern myself too much if I were you, Marianne," she said. "You see, I know a little bit more about

47

this child's background than you do. It's small wonder she would want the Blessed Mother to love her particularly. Her own mother is little better than a—a woman of the streets, if you understand my meaning."

Marianne nodded, blushing, not so much from embarrassment over the subject of conversation as from embarrassment over Sister Anne-Marie's evident embarrassment.

"This sort of thing happens at times to children Guinevere's age," Sister Anne-Marie went on. "Piety and imagination and the wish to be recognized as somebody of value combine to give the child an experience which to her is wholly real. I do not mean to say that Our Lady and the saints do not show themselves at times to certain privileged people. But in her wisdom our holy mother the Church approaches any claims of this sort with great caution."

She pressed Marianne's hand. "I'm pleased that you're taking an interest in the child. A little honest human friendship is probably what she needs most."

The second bell sounded and Marianne fled to history class, happy to leave her burden behind her in the library. Sister Anne-Marie locked the library and hurried with all dignified speed to the seventh grade classroom, attempting to push the newly acquired burden aside. It was not her way to brood and puzzle over problems which she saw as abstract or beyond her understanding. She was no theologian, and was not the least tempted to tackle any of the more perplexing questions of her religion. The advice she had given Marianne reflected her own attitude. The Church was wiser than she, let the Church decide what it was safe for the faithful to believe. Besides, the business at hand was not strange goings-on in a lonely child's imagination, but compound-complex sentences. Yet even as she led the class in an invocation to the Holy Ghost to inspire their compound-complex sentences, she began to feel a great weight upon her mind wearying and distracting her. But, what if . . . ?

During the long dinner hour, after she had completed her refectory duties, Sister Anne-Marie wandered into the senior homeroom, where Sister Helen was preparing herself for an afternoon of varying levels of Latin. Now that she had not even the diversion of teaching, Sister Anne-Marie was feeling the weight of the burden keenly. It wasn't just another Catechism question with its carefully worded Catechism answer; it wasn't just another improbable anecdote from the *Lives of the Saints*. It was something happening now and, what was worse, here. Sister Anne-Marie was a person of vicarious tastes; she preferred to be thrilled by imaginary exploits in books than to dare the roller-coaster ride herself, and she preferred to experience the presence of Divinity from a proper and safe Sacramental distance to confronting her Lord face to face in some earthly garden.

Sister Helen looked up with a parody of a smile. In spite of the differences between them in age and temperament the two nuns were close friends.

"Hello, dear. Something on your mind?" With the casual rudeness of familiarity Sister Helen returned her attention to her lesson plan. But Sister Anne-Marie was not to be put off. She needed to talk badly. She pulled up a chair onto the platform and sat beside Sister Helen.

"How's *The Wizard* going?"

Sister Helen snorted. "Don't ask. It's a sore point." She did not bother to look up from the lesson plan. Sister Anne-Marie could think of no other topic of conversation except that which she was trying to keep to herself. She lapsed into silence, watching Sister Helen make marginal notes on Virgil's syntax. It was too bad they had to do that sort of thing, mutilating poetry with marginal notes or dissecting beautifully constructed sentences and labeling them with ugly double-barreled names like compound-complex.

"It's an awful thing to say, Sister," she mused, "but I'm not at all sure that I approve of teaching."

"That's because you're young and believe all the claptrap in the education textbooks. I've been teaching for twenty years now. It's a gesture. I go through a formula, throw words at them. They take tests, try to throw the words back at me.

49

Some of them are good at it and collect honors and go to college to have longer words thrown at them. Others aren't so good. A few can't do it at all and after a while give up. Rarely, very, very rarely the words fall in a fertile place and produce fruit. But not often. It should come as a surprise when it does happen. One ought not to expect it as a matter of course." She continued making marks in the text of her Virgil, underlining phrases and circling words as she spoke. "Teaching can be a very discouraging job if you allow it to get to you. It never comes up to expectations, but then most jobs don't. At least in teaching you have a chance for that rare thing to happen."

She closed her book and leaned back in her chair.

"Now, dear, what's really on your mind?"

Because she could no longer tolerate it Sister Anne-Marie gave in and thrust the burden onto Sister Helen's well-fleshed shoulders. Sister Helen threw it down with an operatic laugh. She had been trained for the lyric stage in her distant youth and tended to revert occasionally to the mannerisms of the theater, especially when angry or amused.

"That pale little thing that hangs around with Tootsie Palmisano? Come, Sister, don't let your imagination carry you off. I'm sure Our Blessed Lady, if she wished to honor earth with a visit, could find a more appropriate landing place than this convent and a more inspiring object for her conversation than Guinevere d'Arblay."

Sister Anne-Marie flushed. "The same could be said for Joan of Arc or the children of Fatima or—or St. Dorothea."

Sister Helen patted her arm. "I'm not trying to belittle you, dear, but I'm sure there's no good reason for taking such a contention from such a child with any seriousness whatsoever. Beware of making too much of the trivial." Laughing, she pointed to the Latin motto she had lettered on the blackboard behind her desk for the edification of her advanced seniors:

Parturient montes, nascetur ridiculus mus.

Sister Anne-Marie also laughed. It was always good to talk

to Sister Helen. Her tough worldliness was just the splash of vinegar Sister Anne-Marie sometimes needed. As the period bell rang she set out for an hour of study hall monitoring with a high heart, joyfully leaving the burden behind, discarded like yesterday's lecture notes on Sister Helen's platform.

It did not lie there long. Midway through the third book of *The Aeneid* Sister Helen saw the pallid face of Guinevere d'Arblay rise before her like an unbidden ghost. The sight unnerved Sister Helen, who by nature was very difficult to unnerve.

"What do you want?" she asked sharply.

"Sister Stephanie sent me with these." The apparition placed in Sister Helen's hand a very real packet of printed papers. The programs for *The Wizard of Oz*. Sister Helen grasped them, relieved. It was only an ordinary child on an ordinary errand. But before dismissing the messenger Sister Helen looked hard into her face. It was such a thoroughly open face, painful in its naïveté and free from any suggestion of either duplicity or of emotional disturbance.

"Thank you, Guinevere. Tell Sister Stephanie thank you for me."

"Yes, Sister."

"And go straight back to your room. No dawdling in the yard."

"Oh no, Sister."

The blue eyes were wide and innocent. For the first time Sister Helen was distracted by a great "what if?" It was beyond belief, but then most of the things her religion required her to believe were like that. Reluctantly Sister Helen took up the burden Sister Anne-Marie had left on the platform, settling it on her shoulders as comfortably as possible.

About ten minutes into the second period, a hopeless struggle with the unpredictable genders of third declension nouns, Sister Helen surrendered, gave the class a written assignment, put one of the trustworthy girls in charge and went down to the superior's office.

"I hope I'm not bothering you with trivia, Mother, but a

matter has come to my attention that you might want to consider investigating."

It was a rather dry and formal statement, safe in its legalistic terminology, but it represented the transfer of a burden, to the relief of Sister Helen, who gladly fled back to third declension nouns, and to the consternation of Mother Ignatius, who now had one more problem to deal with.

She recalled with bitter amusement a discussion she had once had with a Confirmation class. She had been explaining the holiness of the bishop's office and the importance of Apostolic succession. Every bishop in the Church, she had explained, was a direct successor to one of Our Lord's Apostles, the first bishops. For this reason every priest must desire the holy honor of being consecrated bishop. An open-faced girl had raised her hand to ask if every nun's ambition was to be a superior. And she could not understand why Mother Ignatius laughed so.

Mother Ignatius had spent the early part of the afternoon trying to iron out some of the difficulties spawned by the temporary appointment of a recent college graduate from the town to replace Sister Clementine. It was always open season on lay teachers at a convent school, and this one was also young, inept and Methodist. Mother Ignatius was trying to make do with her just until the end of the term, when it would be unnecessary to dismiss her since, like most young, inept town girls, she was getting married. In the meantime Mother Ignatius' main concern was keeping the lid on. Today, for example, she had had to endure an hour-and-a-half harangue from the mother of a student who had been disciplined for taking part in a spitball incident.

"Oh, Mother, you don't know how humiliated I am," the woman had wailed. "I told her it's bad enough getting caught throwing spitballs—but at a Protestant, that's too much."

Mother Ignatius had hardly had time to recover from that visit when Sister Helen burst into her office with some wild tale about heavenly apparitions at the Shrine. Of course, being Sister Helen, she had made it sound about as wild as a monthly financial report. But Mother Ignatius was not fooled. She had been around long enough to recognize a wild tale when she heard one. She did her best to reassure Sister Helen and indicated her intention to investigate. Then she sat alone in her office, examining with deliberation the size, shape and contents of the burden that had been dumped on her.

She half envied the young lay teacher who had nothing to worry about but spitballs and weddings. But it was a different matter to be confronted with a possible major miracle on her own doorstep, afraid to accept it in case it was false and reluctant to reject it in case it was genuine. That is the heavy price the believer pays for his faith, this agonizing uncertainty that troubles not the happy agnostic. She could not afford to dismiss this girl's claim out of hand as merely a manifestation of hysteria or a lonely child's conscious bid for attention, but neither could she afford to embrace the miracle unquestioningly.

It did not take Mother Ignatius long to realize that the burden was more than she could cope with. She was used to burdens and knew well how to analyze them. This particular burden was certainly not meant for her. It must be passed on at once into consecrated hands. She rose quickly from her desk and made for the hall. By the grace of God she confronted Father Kelly leaving the junior homeroom.

"Could I trouble you for a moment, Father?"

It WAS the first Friday in May, and every First Friday afternoon the convent population and a few faithful old ladies assembled in the church of Our Lady, Star of the Sea for Rosary and Benediction. Sister Helen at the organ was modulating and improvising impatiently, for the clergy had failed to appear in the chancel on time. Monsignor Fulham stood in the sacristy, vested and visibly annoyed, as Father Kelly rushed in looking dazed.

"Father, I've got to talk to you. Something remarkable has happened."

"It can wait until after Benediction," Monsignor Fulham

snapped. "I'm going to start the Rosary. You get vested and join me in the chancel double quick."

Manrico Palmisano exchanged a surreptitious grin with his fellow altar boy. It wasn't often one had the privilege of hearing grown-ups in authority getting bawled out.

Sister Helen played the organ and led the singing, simple, happy, uncomplicated hymns to the Virgin filled with the light of stars and the flowers of May. Monsignor Fulham led the recitation of the Rosary with the belated assistance of Father Kelly, who seemed strangely preoccupied and kept losing count of the "Hail Marys." The Grand Finale was Benediction of the Blessed Sacrament. Manny Palmisano filled the church with the mystic odor of incense, and the nuns, students and old ladies sang St. Thomas' great songs of awed worship and tender affection:

"O salutaris Hostia
Quae coeli pandis ostium. . . ."

Monsignor Fulham, enburdened with a richly embroidered cope, took from its sanctuary the gold-rayed monstrance, raised it amidst the fanfare of incense and bells, turned about and held it over the black and blue congregation of nuns and uniformed children, who bowed in humble, silent adoration before the thing the monstrance held: a thin circle of white bread upon which a miracle had been worked. Monsignor Fulham bowed his knee and worshiped that remarkable piece of bread before replacing it in the curtained sanctuary. There was a rustle throughout the church like a communal sigh of relief that the Presence of God was now a little less immediate.

Monsignor Fulham spoke the litany in a firm voice, the people repeating after him:

"Blessed be God
Blessed be His Holy Name. . . ."

After pronouncing in this manner approval of the Persons of the Trinity, the Blessed Virgin, the patient Joseph and an

54

extensive list of saints and angels, Monsignor Fulham concluded with a sentence borrowed from Our Lady's litany:

"Star of the Sea, pray for us."

The organ sounded triumphantly human chords, and the black and blue congregation sang with enthusiasm the stirring finale of this sacred pantomine:

"Holy God we praise Thy Name!
Lord of all we bow before Thee!
All on earth Thy sceptre claim,
All in heaven above adore Thee.
Infinite Thy vast domain.
Everlasting is Thy Reign!"

Once they had changed from the medieval finery of church vestments to the somewhat less exotic costume of black cassock and Roman collar, and the altar boys had been sent shouting on their way, Monsignor Fulham questioned Father Kelly about his agitation.

"So now, Father, suppose you tell me just what's eating you."

Father Kelly was delighted to toss into Monsignor Fulham's unsuspecting lap the burden that Mother Ignatius had so gently and tactfully passed on to him. Monsignor Fulham collapsed under its weight, for of all those who had handled it that day, he alone fully appreciated it. He sank into a chair, holding his head.

"Holy Mother of God!"

"Yes," Father Kelly cried exultant. "Exactly. Nobody less than the Holy Mother of God herself comes traipsing down from the highest heaven to visit our little Shrine. Just think of it."

Monsignor Fulham rose heavily. He had no one to pass the burden on to and had no idea how he could deal with it himself.

"Think of it all you like, Father. But you are not to speak of this matter, not to anyone, until it has been fully investigated. Do you understand? You are to say nothing to anyone."

"All right, Father. I won't. But I must say you are responding strangely to such a great blessing being laid upon us all."

He held the door open for his pastor. As they stepped out into the smothering heat of May, Monsignor Fulham slapped to death a mosquito humming in his ear.

"I think it wisest, Father, to hold back our rejoicing until we have made certain whether what we have here is a blessing or a curse or, as is most likely, something considerably less than either."

He preceded Father Kelly into the rectory, to be greeted by the comforting aroma of freshly caught speckled trout frying in butter.

7

Saturday Morning. Lazy and peaceful, the convent dozed in the May heat. Nuns and boarders puttered about on their assigned Saturday tasks: changing beds, sorting laundry, sweeping, dusting, polishing. Monsignor Fulham paced the cement yard in front of the church, mumbling at his breviary and glancing every few minutes toward the path from the convent. He was expecting a visitor, for so it had been arranged with Mother Ignatius. She planned to send the child over on some pretext so that he might discreetly question her. As he went back into the rectory to prepare for this rather touchy interview, he was annoyed to find Father Kelly loitering in the hall outside the pastor's office.

"Haven't you work to do this morning, Father?" Monsignor Fulham inquired testily.

"You're going to talk to the little girl who sees Our Lady, aren't you?" Father Kelly said with painful eagerness.

"Yes, Father. Privately. That is why I am here. Can you as easily explain your presence? Are you perhaps expecting to gain a plenary indulgence from touching the hem of her uniform?"

Father Kelly turned away angry and started to walk out. Then he thought better of it, turned about again and followed his superior into his cluttered office.

"Don't you see, Father," he pleaded, extending his hands in a gesture of Gaelic supplication, "if Our Lady has in truth come to earth it must be for some wondrous purpose. She may be bringing a message of salvation for man. Why shouldn't I want to be among the first to hear it?"

Monsignor Fulham sighed very slowly and very loudly. He sat at his overladen desk and began sorting through a pile of papers and documents.

"Ah," he cried, seizing a typewritten sheet and waving it triumphantly in front of Father Kelly. "Here is a list of the candidates for Confirmation. Go through the register and make sure that the records of their Baptism and First Communion are all in proper order."

Father Kelly took the paper reluctantly.

"Now?"

"Yes, Father. Now. If there is a message for you I'll see that it's delivered."

Dragging his feet like a child sent early to bed, Father Kelly left. Monsignor Fulham sat staring absently at the palm tree outside his window and contemplated the best way of approaching the difficult matter before him.

There was a timid tap on his office door.

"Come in, please," Monsignor Fulham called.

Guinevere d'Arblay entered holding gingerly in one hand a large bundle of Sodality medals on wide powder blue ribbons.

"Excuse me, Father. Mother Ignatius would like you to bless these for her, please."

"Certainly, Guinevere," said Monsignor Fulham. "I'll be glad to."

She held the medals out to him. He drew a cross in the air above them and muttered the threefold Latin names of God.

"Now," he said. "If you have a few minutes to spare maybe you'd like to sit down and tell me all about how you're doing here."

The child hesitated, looking at the medals dangling from her hand and then at the priest.

"Is that all there is to it?"

"That's all," Monsignor Fulham smiled. "God in His mercy has made His blessings fairly easy to come by. Here, speaking of blessings, I have a little gift for you."

Reaching into a desk drawer, he pulled out a chain of blue beads with a small silver crucifix hanging pendant from it. The priest took care that the child did not see that in the drawer there were about twenty others just like it.

"A rosary," she cried. "Oh, how nice. I've been wanting one."

"It was blessed by the Holy Father himself."

"Oh." Guinevere's eyes widened. "Is there a Holy Father, too? I know the Holy Mother. She likes to talk to me when I visit her at the Shrine. She says it's all right to talk to you about her now that it's out in the open. I don't know what that means. She told me this morning. She says that you are a very good man and have lots of sense. But I'm not supposed to talk to Father Kelly about her. She says he's a good man, too, but he suffers from enthusiasm. I don't know what that means either."

Monsignor Fulham rose quickly and turned to the window for fear that his face would reveal both his surprise at the ease of his conquest and his amusement at this accurate appraisal of his curate.

"So," he said slowly. "Our Lady talks to you at the Shrine. Does she talk to anyone else?"

"No, Father, just me. And only when I'm by myself."

"Why?"

"I don't know, Father. I guess she just wants to talk to me."

"And why does she want to talk to you in particular? Has she told you that?"

"Oh yes, Father. It's because I need mothering."

"Oh," Monsignor Fulham murmured weakly. "So that's it." It certainly wasn't the sort of thing he was expecting. A strange fantasy, if that's what it was.

"She talks to me and I talk to her," the child went on eagerly. "I don't always understand what she means. I'm not exactly a brain, you know. She told me the funniest thing the other day. I was kind of down, not having too many friends and all, and I said, 'What can I do?' and she said, 'Follow the Yellow Brick Road.' Just like Jennie says in the play. I don't know what she meant, but that's all she would tell me.

"Oh, and she helps me with things, lessons and stuff. She's teaching me the prayers." Guinevere looked down at the rosary in her hand. "She taught me the 'Hail Mary.' That's her favorite. You say it once for every little bead, right?"

"Right," Monsignor Fulham replied, breathing a silent prayer to the Holy Spirit for guidance. "And you say the 'Our Father' on the big beads. Has she taught you the 'Our Father'?"

Guinevere nodded. "I don't have it all right yet. It's longer than the 'Hail Mary' and the words are harder. She says you don't have to know what the words mean, but I like knowing what they mean. I like the part about daily bread. I'm a good eater." She smiled at him proudly. It was the first time he'd seen her smile.

Reaching into another desk drawer, Monsignor Fulham pulled out a box of pralines, a delicacy of the region: an incredibly rich sugar candy baked in flat beige pancakes garnished with large pieces of papershell pecan.

"In that case I reckon you know what to do with this," Monsignor Fulham said, offering his guest a praline.

"Oh, thank you, Father. This is much better than bread."

Monsignor Fulham sat forward, leaning over the desk toward her.

"What about the last part of the 'Our Father,' Guinevere? Has she taught you that?"

The child thought a moment, chewing on her praline. "Let's see, 'daily bread, forgive us our trespasses as we forgive those who—' Oh yes. I've got it now. 'Lead us not into temptation but deliver us from evil, amen.' I understand about evil, but I don't know what temptation is."

"Oh, that's very important. Temptation is the devil's work, making evil look like good so that we fall into sin. Do you know about the devil, Guinevere?"

She nodded. "Oh yes. Sister Stephanie talks a lot about the devil making kids talk in class and stuff."

"He's capable of far worse than that, my dear. He is the evil we pray Our Father to deliver us from. See?"

He printed the word DEVIL on his memo pad, then circled the last four letters and set the pad in front of her.

"Gee," Guinevere breathed, fascinated by this little word game. "I never noticed."

"He's very clever, the devil," Monsignor Fulham persisted. "He can do almost anything he wants. He can change his looks and his voice, make you think he's God or a saint or even Our Blessed Lady herself. He has tricked many good people into sin that way."

"Oh." Guinevere stared at her rosary, looking a little puzzled. Then she laughed. "Now I see. You think she's— Oh no, Father, she's the Star of the Sea, she's all good. You'd never think such a thing if you met her."

"But I haven't met her. No one has met her but you." He grasped her hand. "You are a very good little girl. I should not want you to be led into temptation. You think about it and pray to Our Father to lead us all to the truth, all right? Now when you go back to the convent tell Mother Ignatius that I shall be over around three this afternoon to discuss the matter she wanted to talk to me about. And you come to see me soon again, will you?"

He walked with her to the door of the rectory and watched her skip guilelessly down the path to the convent, his heart far from easy. He was deeply provoked on turning back to his office to be accosted by Father Kelly.

"What does Our Lady want, Father? Is there a message?"

Monsignor Fulham gave his young colleague a withering look.

"Our Lady is of the opinion that you suffer from enthusiasm, Father."

61

The young priest lowered his eyes. Monsignor Fulham walked over to the door of his office.

"But the message." Father Kelly's voice was anxious, almost childishly shrill with disappointment. "What's the message?"

"Follow the Yellow Brick Road."

Monsignor Fulham went into his office and closed the door firmly behind him.

EVERY SATURDAY afternoon the boarding students went to the movies. But this particular Saturday, Marianne Brandon remained behind, for Mother Ignatius had asked her to take part in a very small private conference being held in the nuns' common room at the rear of the second floor. Besides those who had shared Friday's burden, Sister Stephanie was present, for being Guinevere's teacher, she might prove helpful. Mother Ignatius had felt it wise to include Sister Clementine as well.

Marianne carefully and diligently recounted the events of Thursday night, and Monsignor Fulham described the interview in his office that morning. Sister Stephanie, the only member of the conference to whom all this was new, sat silently pursing her lips and now and then shaking her head. But when Monsignor Fulham, much to his curate's embarrassment, repeated the comment on Father Kelly's enthusiasm she could no longer contain herself.

"No," she said sharply. "But no. She just isn't capable of it, that one. Oh, she's a good little girl, to be sure, and I get few enough of them in my room. Straight 'A' in deportment she'll get from me, but certainly not in anything else. She could never have made a statement like that herself. Her vocabulary is limited to one-syllable words."

"But Our Lady could have put the words in her mouth," Father Kelly challenged. "It just shows that the vision is genuine."

"No, Father, I'm afraid it doesn't," said Monsignor Fulham. "Obviously the child got the statement from somewhere other than her own head. But that's no reason to jump to the conclusion that it had heavenly inspiration."

"Nor to conclude that it didn't," Sister Clementine muttered sulkily. She made it plain by the set of her shoulders that she in no way approved of the proceedings.

"You believe then that this child has actually seen and spoken to Our Lady, Sister?" Monsignor Fulham asked.

"Yes, Father. Not that I expect you to pay any attention to what a silly old woman thinks. But I know that Shrine better than any of you, and I've always known she was there."

"Have you ever seen her yourself, Sister?" asked Mother Ignatius. "Has she ever spoken to you?"

Sister Clementine shook her head. "No, Mother. But I know she's there. I talk to her."

"Doesn't it make you wonder that she would show herself to a strange child and not to you who have served her so faithfully all these years?"

Sister Clementine stuck out her bony chin proudly.

"That's the way Our Blessed Mother wants it. And whatever she wants is all right with me. This affair is just between her and little Guinevere. Our Blessed Mother doesn't want the rest of us snooping about."

"How can you be so sure?" Sister Helen asked.

"She told Guinevere," Sister Clementine replied firmly. "And Guinevere told me. And why not? Our Blessed Mother doesn't always need a reason for what she does. It's different when she's sent, you see, with a message from heaven or some such. But then it isn't her affair at all, it's His. She isn't interested in doctrine and politics and things like that. But she is interested in children. That seems obvious."

"Hmm." Monsignor Fulham stroked the midday stubble on his chin. "This is all most interesting. I don't believe I've come across these particular Marian doctrines in my extensive reading."

"Some things you don't have to read in books, Father," Sister Clementine sniffed. "Some things you just understand. With all respect, Monsignor, I wonder if it isn't just a little

63

presumptuous of you-all to assume that Our Blessed Mother has to do what all the theologians expect her to. Don't you think she has a mind of her own?"

"Bravo!" Marianne whispered. Only Sister Helen heard the comment, and she said nothing, but made a mental note of the interesting outburst. She wasn't fond of Marianne, for she had a secret aversion to "good girls," not having been one herself. But there was something in this reaction that she did like.

"It just makes no sense to me," Sister Stephanie grumbled. "The world is full of motherless children. Why settle on this one, who isn't even strictly motherless at all? Consider all the orphanages in France . . ." Her sentence trailed off unfinished but filled with the implication that a worthier candidate could easily be found in one of those French orphanages.

"I don't see what you have against this child," Sister Clementine complained. "She is as polite and well spoken as any of your fine French children. She is partly French, anyway, I think."

"Creole," Sister Stephanie sniffed.

"None of your purebred French girls would be so devoted to the Shrine." Sister Clementine's voice rose querulously. "Our Blessed Mother has a right to be nice to any little girl she wants to!"

"Sisters, Sisters," Mother Ignatius interposed quickly. "Let us not lose sight of the true nature of our inquiry. I suppose we could concede for the sake of argument that the comforting of a lonely child is legitimate cause for Our Lady to come down from heaven."

"I'm not about to concede any such thing," Sister Helen laughed. "Not even, begging your pardon, Mother, for the sake of argument. Besides, if that's all there is to it, why all the secrecy?"

"Because of the camellias," Sister Clementine responded promptly. "When a lot of people find out she's been someplace they all come crowding around looking for miracles and ruin the gardens." She regarded them all with a look of cool triumph. "Only Our Blessed Mother herself could show that kind of concern for my camellias."

"Oh, come, Sister," Sister Anne-Marie cried. "This is absurd. The child obviously dreamed the whole thing up."

"Not likely," Sister Stephanie sniffed. "She has no imagination, that one, and very little intelligence. Besides, I don't think she's really capable of deceit."

"You're right about that, Sister," Monsignor Fulham agreed. "I'm quite certain she believes in these visions or whatever herself. But that doesn't preclude the possibility of self-deceit or hallucination or even some diabolical manifestation."

Sister Helen sighed loudly.

"Oh, for goodness' sake. What would the devil want with Guinevere d'Arblay?"

"What he wants with all of us, Sister."

"But how do we find out the truth?" asked Sister Anne-Marie.

"How, indeed," replied Monsignor Fulham. "This is the question I have spent the morning praying and struggling over. I don't believe there is really very much else we can do at this point but pray and struggle."

"We could ask for a sign," said Father Kelly.

"Signs and wonders are easily come by, and Satan can supply them as easily as the saints. The absence of a sign need not prove the absence of a true vision but only might indicate Our Lady's disapproval of our insistence upon one. We must be patient."

"Do you think it would be wise to discourage the child from visiting the Shrine?" asked Mother Ignatius.

"Yes," said Monsignor Fulham. "So long as she is not aware that she is being deliberately prevented from pursuing her activities. If she can be diverted, gotten interested in other things, she just might abandon the whole business herself. If she is happy she might no longer need Our Lady's mothering. Is there some way of keeping most of her free time occupied and supervised for a while?"

"She promised me she wouldn't go to the Shrine at night anymore," said Marianne. "I'm sure she'll keep her word."

"After school she always comes to rehearsal," said Sister Helen. "That will keep her occupied at least until the show."

"What about recess and after lunch?" Mother Ignatius asked. "Is there something she might take an interest in, like sports, or maybe art?"

"She's no good at sports," Sister Stephanie sighed. "And she can't draw. I tell you the child is a nondescript. She has no talent and very few interests." She smiled pensively. "I remember when I was a schoolgirl in Marseilles there was a child who claimed to see angels during the Elevation. Every morning after Mass she was asked if she had seen them. Every time she said she had she was soundly thrashed. After two weeks she didn't see them anymore."

Monsignor Fulham turned on the superior an astonished look. He was less familiar than the convent community with Sister Stephanie's flagellant fantasies. Mother Ignatius sent him a reassuring wink.

"It is not the custom at the Convent of the Holy Innocents to make use of such methods, Sister, so I suggest you concentrate on more acceptable solutions."

Sister Stephanie frowned, smarting under the rebuke. Then she brightened suddenly.

"I know one thing she is interested in. She wants to make her First Communion."

"Yes, yes, of course!" Monsignor Fulham exclaimed. "And she ought to. She's almost old enough for Confirmation. Send her over to my office at recess Monday, and I'll begin her instruction at once. It'll give me something of an opportunity to work with her discreetly on this other matter."

"Very good," said Mother Ignatius, folding her hands. "That takes care of everything except the period between lunch and supper, and we'll just all have to do what we can to keep her occupied then. If she should wander down to the Shrine, Sister Clementine could divert her. I trust I can count on your cooperation in this matter, Sister?"

Sister Clementine nodded. "Of course, Mother. I'm not so old and dotty that I've forgotten my vow of obedience to my superiors. Anyhow, I'm curious to see what happens. Our Blessed Mother isn't likely to be thwarted so easily."

"What about Jennie and Tootsie?" asked Sister Stephanie. "They seem to know all about this business, anyway. I could get them to watch her."

"Oh no," cried Marianne. "That'd never do. They're best friends. They'd tell her right away what we're doing. There's nothing more sacred to kids that age than best friends."

"I hadn't thought of that," said Mother Ignatius. "Thank you, Marianne. It is helpful having a representative of the opposition on the panel, isn't it?"

She rose, indicating that the conference was over. She thanked the priests for giving their time and assured them that they would be kept informed.

All walked together down to the main staircase.

Father Kelly sighed. "I suppose you are taking the right approach, Father, but it does seem a shame to have the ear of heaven hovering so close and just turn away."

Monsignor Fulham smiled at Mother Ignatius.

"Father Kelly's in the market for a divine message or at least a minor miracle."

"Oh, as far as that goes," the superior replied, smiling gently at the young priest, "I'm sure we all have some secret wish we'd like to be sure reached heaven's ear. Sister Clementine wants a new statue, of course, and Sister Stephanie is just dying to get back to France, where all the children are civilized. What would you whisper into the ear of heaven if you got the chance, Sister Anne-Marie? What is your wish?"

Sister Anne-Marie pursed her lips a moment, thinking. It was such a nuisance, all this uncertainty. She felt just a little put out that the Church hadn't provided a sure and unequivocal answer to all this nonsense.

"The Truth," she declared with sudden firmness. "That's my wish—a certain glimpse of Truth!"

Sister Helen laughed. "That's an ambitious one. And not

one I should care at all for. I lack the courage to confront bare Truth. It would surely destroy me. I feel safer going on faith. No, my desires are much more pragmatic. I wish only to get through this blasted play decently."

They all laughed, somewhat relieved to have the matter reduced to a parlor game.

"But, mind you, one warning," Sister Helen added with a show of seriousness. "If there is any truth in the old folk tales, getting wishes granted is a hazardous business. Remember what happened to the woodcutter and his wife."

The others stopped in mid-descent of the staircase, looking back expectantly toward Sister Helen standing at the railing above.

"Oh, you know the story. The woodcutter did some favor for the local dryad and was granted three wishes as a reward. He and his wife went into a long consultation over how they could get the most out of this chance, but they argued too long, and the woodcutter became hungry. Without thinking, he wished he had a nice fat sausage for supper, and immediately there one was on the kitchen table. The wife fell into a great rage and berated and nagged the poor woodcutter for wasting a precious wish on so common and insignificant an item until he finally lost his temper, cursed her roundly and wished the sausage hung from the end of her nose."

"Ah-ha," said Monsignor Fulham. "A just reward for shrewish wives. Too bad he didn't use his last wish to make himself wealthy for life and leave his wife to cope with her sausage as best she could. But they're always an ethical lot, these woodcutters."

"And loyal to their greedy wives," Sister Helen added. "So he used his last wish to extricate the sausage from his wife's nose. They had it for supper and lived happily ever after. So be warned and watch your step, all you wishers."

As the group separated at the foot of the stairs, Mother Ignatius laid her hand on the pastor's sleeve.

"Are you planning to report this matter to the Bishop, Father?" she whispered.

"Not at present," Monsignor Fulham hedged. "Are you planning to report it to your Provincial?"

Mother Ignatius dropped her eyes. Monsignor Fulham smiled.

"I suspect, Reverend Mother," he said softly, "that your secret wish is rather similar to mine."

"No more headaches, Monsignor. That's all I ask. No more headaches."

"Amen," said Monsignor Fulham.

8

WHEN SHE was not teaching English or Latin or keeping her senior homeroom in working order, Sister Helen attempted to teach music. For one hour a week in the period before noon students were assembled in large chunks in the music room on the second floor of the new elementary building. Monday was music day for the middle elementary chunk—grades four, five and six. Sister Helen had somewhat arbitrarily divided the girls into sopranos and altos, mostly for the purpose of introducing the idea of part singing and attempting a few rounds. Being allowed only an hour a week to teach the rudiments of music, she had been unable to take the time to test voices. At first she had simply let the students decide for themselves where their voices lay. This policy resulted in a badly unbalanced choir since for some reason quite beyond Sister Helen's comprehension no one wanted to admit to being an alto. So Sister Helen was forced to draft most of the alto section.

At this time she was teaching the middle elementaries the *Panis Angelicus* by rote since very few could read music. First she took them through it a number of times all together. With its wealth of sustained sibilants the hymn was a rather dreadful piece to attempt on an untrained choir, and it usually degenerated into a bedlam of random hisses.

While Sister Helen was taking the sopranos separately, the altos whispered and nudged each other behind her back.

"All right now!" she exclaimed, spinning around suddenly on the disruptive altos. "Since you-all are so full of sound this morning, let's see how you sing it on your own. First verse. Altos only—one, two . . ."

From the startled and unprepared altos came, as she had expected, only a low, jumbled murmur and, as she had not expected, one delicate, bell-clear voice:

"*Panis angelicus, fit panis Dominum.* . . ."

The voice wavered, realizing that it sang alone.

"Go on," Sister Helen said. The voice continued, pure and true to the end of the verse:

"*O res mirabilis, manducat hominum.*
Pauper, servus et humilis."

"Thank you, Guinevere. That was lovely. You have a beautiful voice."

"Thank you, Sister." Guinevere blushed bright red and then winced, for Brenda Sue Foote, who was standing just behind her, had driven the tip of a mechanical pencil into her ribs.

"Now that we have had a solo rendition," Sister Helen said, "I should like to hear from all the altos. Keep your 's's' together and hold the vowels for the full count. 'Pa-nees ahnjail-icoos.' One, two . . ."

Brenda Sue waited until Sister Helen's back was turned before once more making use of her pencil as an instrument of torture. This time her victim turned about and gave her one of those long, searching looks with which she often responded to Brenda Sue's little acts of persecution.

"That kid gives me the creeps," Brenda Sue whispered loudly.

Sister Helen turned slowly to face the alto section, her face stormy.

"One solo performance is sufficient, Guinevere. You will remain after class."

71

"It wasn't Gwen that talked, Sister," blurted out Jennie, who had been watching the exchange in helpless anger from the soprano section. "It was Brenda Sue Foote, the two-faced sneak."

"Would you like to spend your dinner hour singing duets with your friend, Jennifer?" Sister Helen asked.

"No, Sister."

"Very well, then, unless I ask your assistance in maintaining discipline in this class, you would be wise to remain silent."

"Yes, Sister."

The bell sounded, the Angelus was said and all the class except Guinevere silently marched out. The instant her feet touched the dust of the school yard, Jennie tackled Brenda Sue hard from behind, knocking her flat and falling heavily on top of her.

"Sorry, honey," she shouted. "I slipped on a banana peel." But in Brenda Sue's ear she quickly whispered, "If I ever catch you messing with my best friend, I'll knock your ugly block off. Is that clear?"

The music room was suddenly empty and eerily quiet. As if from another existence the screams and shouts of the liberated children drifted through the open window. Sister Helen gently closed the door and turned to face the child still standing in her place in the alto section staring down at her scuffed and dirty saddle oxfords. Sister Stephanie was right; the child was as nondescript and colorless as her wilting blue uniform. And yet, unless Sister Helen had been hallucinating, an unspeakably beautiful sound had come forth from the child's nondescript throat.

Sister Helen walked over to the piano and struck a C-major chord.

"Sing 'Ah.' "

Guinevere sang "Ah." Sister Helen had not been hallucinating. She took the child up the scale until her voice broke.

"I'm sorry, Sister. I can't sing that high."

Sister Helen laughed. "Oh yes you can, when you learn to do it right. Tell me, dear, do you like to sing?"

72

"Oh yes, Sister. I love to, but sometimes I don't sound right."

"I could teach you to sing properly, if you are interested," Sister Helen said slowly, looking hard at the girl.

"Would you really?" Guinevere cried, her eyes bright.

"Only if you are willing to work very hard and give up your free time to it."

A shadow crossed Guinevere's face and she hesitated.

"Oh dear. I'm so busy now I never seem to have any time for . . ." She walked slowly over to the window and stared out beyond the crowded, screaming playground and the grove of trees toward the cupola roof of the Shrine. Sister Helen stared hard into the back of her head.

"Yes," Guinevere said slowly, turning back into the room. "It's a good idea. I can come and learn to sing. I'll work very hard for you. I think I'd like to do that."

Sister Helen closed the piano and started for the door.

"All right. We'll meet here then this afternoon after play practice. Shall we go to dinner now?"

"But, Sister, I thought you were keeping me in."

"Oh yes. I was going to keep you in for talking in class, wasn't I?"

"Yes, Sister."

Sister Helen took the child by the shoulders and roughly propelled her out of the music room, locking the door behind them.

"Did you talk in class, Guinevere?"

"No, Sister. I never talk in class."

"Then there isn't any point in my keeping you in, is there?"

"No, Sister. I guess not. But I don't understand—"

"If you stand here any longer arguing with me, you're going to miss your dinner. Now trot, double quick!"

Sister Helen gave her a slight push.

"Yes, Sister. Thank you, Sister. Good-bye, Sister."

The child ran bumping down the hall. Sister Helen stood wondering with her hand still on the doorknob. Absurd. That's what it was, absolutely absurd. Still wondering, she walked over to the nuns' refectory, for she did not want to be late for dinner either.

THE SUN SET late in May, and the dark of night followed close on its train, for the subtropic South knew no twilight. Marianne Brandon personally tucked in each of her young charges before turning out the dormitory's overhead lights. She gave Guinevere d'Arblay a sisterly peck on the cheek.

"G'night, punkin. You stay in now, OK?"

"OK, Marianne. I promise." Guinevere closed her eyes. Marianne gently drew the bed curtains together and went to her own bed, where she was permitted to read by a small lamp for another hour.

From under her bedsprings she drew out a familiar-looking book carefully camouflaged in a textbook cover. It had been by chance that she had recognized it sticking slightly out of a trash can waiting to be emptied into the local garbage truck. Sister Anne-Marie had been a little careless in the disposal of this occasion of sin. Marianne was not sure why she had rescued the book, it wasn't a very good story, nor was it particularly well written, but now that she had sinned anyhow by deliberately snatching the justly condemned book from the fire and would have no opportunity to confess until Friday, she supposed she might as well finish reading it and get the whole thing out of her system. She wondered as she listened to the Crescent Limited whistle up the coast what it was really like to be seduced. Well, whatever way she went after graduation, that wasn't an experience she was likely to have. She finished the chapter, returned the book to its hiding place and switched off the light.

THE DISCIPLINE of convent life by its nature left the nuns little time for leisure, but there was the precious hour between students' lights out and the office of Compline, which was the amen of the convent's day. During this wickedly free hour most of the community assembled in the common room reading, talking and occasionally listening to the radio.

Sister Anne-Marie came in from bed check to discover Sister Helen in unnaturally animated conversation with the superior.

"It's incredible, Mother," she was saying. "Simply incredible."

"Good heavens," Sister Anne-Marie said. "Not something else? Isn't there enough incredible activity going on already for one small convent?"

"I've made a discovery, dear," said Sister Helen. "Our little Bernadette has a voice. I mean a real voice. She doesn't know what to do with it, of course, but with proper training she could develop into a top-rate singer."

"And Sister Helen is filling her spare time with voice lessons," added Mother Ignatius. She turned, one headache taken from her, to consult with Sister Stephanie about the arrangements for Guinevere's religious instruction.

"At any rate, there's nothing nondescript about her voice," Sister Helen continued. "With no training at all she has a good range, and I found out this afternoon she's blessed with perfect pitch. Who would have thought it? Such a beautiful sound to come from such an empty head."

Sister Anne-Marie smiled. It was a rare occasion indeed when Sister Helen could be seen to suffer from enthusiasm.

"You weren't wholly honest with us Saturday about your secret wish," she chided. "You really are capable of looking further than next week's show. But you're luckier than the rest of us; you seem to be cashing in on your wishes."

"So I do," Sister Helen murmured. "I suppose I have always wanted a chance to work with real talent. But I was never that much aware of it, to tell the truth. All the same, if I really could have my own way on anything, it wouldn't be Jennie Freret who'd be dancing over the rainbow next Friday night."

EVERY NIGHT before retiring Monsignor Fulham went over to the church for a few minutes alone with his Lord. Walking down the rectory hall, he glanced into the open door of Father Kelly's office. The young priest's dark head was bent over a large book. Monsignor Fulham recognized his own *Lives of the Saints*. Was he still looking for a sign? Monsignor Fulham crept up behind him and looked over his shoulder. The book was opened to the life of St. Catherine, who in her pride refused all suitors as her intellectual inferiors until in a vision the Mother of God appeared to her offering her Divine Son as a suitable bridegroom. Catherine, humbled and finally conquered by love, then devoted all her talents to her husband's business, using her intellect and wit to proselytize until she ended up debating with the local magistrates. Her spirit being uncrushable, her body was mangled instead on the wheel that later gave her name to a delightfully frivolous fireworks device. Monsignor Fulham smiled as he tiptoed out, hoping in his heart that in those final agonizing moments of her life she had been granted a vision of that charming irony. It would have much amused her.

The church was empty and nearly dark. Monsignor Fulham liked it best that way; he couldn't see the gaudy fresco. He knelt before his favorite image, the simple wooden Madonna, and lit a candle, as he did every night. He attached no intention to the candle and spoke but one prayer before it: "Thy will be done." He remained on his knees for some minutes in mindless, unconscious worship. Then he rose wonderfully refreshed and at peace, genuflected before the high altar, blessed himself with holy water at the west door, and walked out quietly to the beach. He stood for some time watching the torches of the flounder fishermen twinkling like stars in the sea, letting the holy water on his forehead dry in the soft wind.

On his way to bed he looked in again on Father Kelly and was amused to find him asleep on St. Francis of Assisi. Monsignor Fulham took out his pen and wrote on the memo pad lying next to the book.

"Follow the Yellow Brick Road."

9

It Was the second Friday in May when, ready or not, the convent's spring show opened for a two-day run. All afternoon throughout the campus tension crackled and discharged in explosive sparks. As the last bell sounded the official close of the school week, day students tore through the school yard like prisoners blessed with sudden amnesty; boarders clustered, pushing in front of the improvised drugstore the nuns had set up across the hall from the basement shower room where they could buy shampoo, soap, bobby pins and stationery on credit. A clutch of girls went over to the church for Confession, hastily slamming blue uniform beanies onto their heads to conform with the Pauline sanctions against the fleshly temptations of uncovered female hair.

Sister Helen met briefly with her cast, limiting her remarks to a few words of encouragement, and sent them all home to rest before evening. Sister Anne-Marie, having left the library temporarily in the charge of a trusted senior, went across the yard to offer her good wishes.

"Well, Jennie," she said, laying her hands on the leading lady's shoulders, "break a leg."

"Huh?" Jennie stared blankly at her.

Both nuns burst into laughter.

"Sister Anne-Marie is making use of a superstition among theatrical people that it is bad luck to wish an actor good luck," Sister Helen explained somewhat obtusely. "So it is good luck to wish you bad luck. See?"

"Yes, Sister," Jennie said uncertainly. To her two inevitable companions she added, "I wish I would."

"Would what?" Guinevere asked.

"Break a leg."

"Gee, what for?"

"So I wouldn't have to do this silly play."

"You mind yourself, Jennie Freret," Sister Helen called sharply. "Go straight home and take a nap. And don't you dare go anywhere near a horse."

"Yes, Sister," Jennie sighed. The girls walked off, arms linked. Sister Anne-Marie returned to the library.

The three best friends walked slowly across the yard to the back gate.

"Do you mean it, Jennie?" Guinevere asked.

"Huh?" said Jennie.

"What you said about breaking your leg. Do you really want to?"

"You bet your bottom dollar," Jennie cried. "I'd do anything to get out of this show. I know I'm gonna make a monkey out of myself. I'm just no good at it. And don't say 'stage fright.' I've ridden in horse shows, and I don't get stage fright. I know what I'm doing on a horse. But this is different. Jeez, I can't even remember my lines. I wish you were doing it, Gwen. You know it better than I do, anyhow."

"But doesn't it hurt, breaking your leg?" Tootsie asked.

"Yeah, I guess so. But it'd be worth it to get out of this stinking show. Anyhow, they give you shots to knock you out."

Tootsie shuddered, being as averse to shots as she was to broken bones. "You better go home like Sister says and take a nap."

After seeing Tootsie off down the road and Jennie into her

mother's station wagon, Guinevere turned back toward the grove of trees. For the first time in nearly two weeks she had a truly free hour. Happily she skipped down the path to the Shrine.

She stopped short, almost stumbling over Sister Clementine, who was on her knees loosening dirt around the rose bushes.

"Hello, honey!" Sister Clementine exclaimed, delicately reinterring an earthworm she had exposed with her trowel. "You haven't been down here for a long time."

"I know," Guinevere said, taking a weeding fork from the nearby wheelbarrow and joining Sister Clementine in the earth. "They keep me busy."

"I bet Our Blessed Mother missed you," Sister Clementine said, giving the child a sidelong glance.

"Do you think so?" Guinevere asked with a thoughtful frown. "I've kind of missed her, too. But I'm happy, like she told me I'd be." She stopped weeding and looked up at the statue. "I have more friends now. Even Sister Helen is my friend, sort of. But the Star of the Sea is still my very best friend. You know what I wish, Sister Clementine? I wish I could be with her all the time. Wouldn't that be nice?"

"Sometimes wishes come true," said Sister Clementine, smiling a little. "Why don't you tell her what you wish and see what happens?"

She rose stiffly and raised her wheelbarrow.

"It's getting hot," she announced in a stilted stage voice. "I think I'll go back to the convent and take a little siesta."

"OK," Guinevere replied. "I'll come up later."

It was a little scene they had played before, and both knew their lines cold.

Guinevere stood at the foot of the Shrine, looking up curiously into the statue's impassive face.

"I just don't get it," she said. "I mean about Jennie wanting to break her leg. Do you get it? I mean if she really wants to, OK, but it sounds nutty to me."

She stopped suddenly, stiff as though listening. Then she said, "Oh phooey. Well, OK. I'll see you later, I hope."

She turned as if in obedience to a command not wholly to her liking and shuffled back up the path toward the deserted school yard. She almost bumped into Sister Helen hurrying down the path toward her.

"Oh, there you are, Guinevere. I've been looking for you. We oughtn't waste a free afternoon like this. You need more work on your breathing."

"Yes, Sister," Guinevere sighed. Scraping her feet in the gray dust of the playground, she followed Sister Helen up to the annex.

"I just can't figure Jennie out, Sister."

"Don't try," said Sister Helen.

GUINEVERE and Sister Helen had been working steadily for nearly an hour on breathing exercises and scales when, knowing well the danger of overworking a young instrument, Sister Helen proposed a change in activity. She began taking various vocal scores from her little library and laying them out in front of her pupil. While she was at it, she figured, she might as well give the child a little grounding in *solfeggio* and basic theory. Professional singers who admitted to being unable to sight-read made Sister Helen ill. She was surprised, considering the girl's general slowness of intellect, how quickly she picked up any knowledge relating to music.

It was Sister Helen's intention not merely to keep Guinevere occupied, but herself as well. She feared for *The Wizard* and wanted to avoid thinking about it as much as possible. It was not that she expected a disaster. Oh no, the show would be well received and would bring in money. But she knew in her heart that it would be an artistic failure. It had just never come alive. Nor was it any use to remind herself that it was her own vanity that was hurting. She might repent of her vanity all she liked, it was as much a part of her as her tendency to put on weight and the thin line of hair on her upper lip. She shuffled through a pile of assorted music sheets.

"Ah, here's something perfect for you!" she exclaimed, setting a sheet of music on the piano. "Come over here and see how you do with this. It's simple and the range is right for you."

She sang softly, and Guinevere followed her:

> "Sweet and low, sweet and low,
>   Wind of the western sea.
>   Low, low, breathe and blow,
>   Wind of the Western sea. . . ."

The music room door opened quietly and Sister Anne-Marie came in. She sat on a chair near the door, and as she often listened in on the lessons, neither Sister Helen nor her pupil took any notice of her.

> "Over the rolling waters flow,
>   Come from the dying moon and blow,
>   Blow him again to me.
>   While my little one,
>   While my pretty one sleeps."

Sister Helen sat back, folding her hands contentedly on her lap.

"Yes, that's very good. It will do splendidly." She smiled kindly on Guinevere. When Sister Helen smiled kindly, which wasn't very often, she looked almost beautiful.

"I used to sing that when I was young," Sister Helen mused. "It's a good piece for a young voice." She looked for the first time at Sister Anne-Marie.

"She sounds good, doesn't she, Sister? Already she's placing her voice better, don't you think?"

Sister Anne-Marie did not reply. For the first time Sister Helen realized that the other nun looked unwell. She was quite pale and appeared nervous to the point of physical tremors, and she stared at Guinevere with a strange, almost terrified expression on her face.

"Look here, dear heart," Sister Helen cried. "Is something the matter?"

"She did it," Sister Anne-Marie whispered. "She just went home and did it." She continued to stare at Guinevere.

81

"If you're trying to tell me something, you're going to have to do a little better than that," Sister Helen urged, trying to keep her voice calm and reasonable. "Now take it slowly, one thing at a time. Who is she, and what did she do?"

Sister Anne-Marie continued to stare at the child standing by the piano and spoke slowly in a toneless voice.

"Jennie Freret broke a leg."

IO

MARIANNE BRANDON walked out of the church of Our Lady, Star of the Sea, blinking at the sudden harsh glare of sunlight, and made for the library. She had finished the improper novel just in time to dispose of it before Confession and had had no difficulty in resolving to avoid this particular sin in the future. The book hadn't been that good; it hadn't even been that titillating. Monsignor Fulham had suggested from the far side of the grate that she satisfy her craving for fiction with the works of some of the many fine Catholic writers.

"I don't suppose you'd go for Chesterton," he had mused. "Sheila Kaye-Smith has written some nice things you might like; historical novels if you crave a bit of adventure, and some fine tales of life in England during the War. But if the English bit doesn't attract you, there's always Kathleen Norris, a trifle romantic for my taste, but probably the perfect thing for the young lady venturing into womanhood. Yes, I'm sure Sister Anne-Marie will have a goodly shelf of Kathleen Norrises. Now mind you, that's not your penance, only a fatherly suggestion. You will say the Rosary and the Way of the Cross for your penance. But don't come back next week without some good Catholic literature under your belt."

Marianne smiled as she mounted the stairs to the rear veranda. It was always a bit of fun to confess to Monsignor Fulham. It was funny how the other girls hadn't caught on. They lined up halfway to the altar rail at Father Kelly's confessional just because he was considered cute. Marianne had tried him a few times and found him severe and inclined to overscold, especially if matters of female purity were involved. She shuddered to think of how he would have responded to her escapade with the naughty novel. Marianne considered what terrible sinners Monsignor Fulham must have absolved in his years in the priesthood to make him so delightfully unimpressed by the transgresssions of convent girls.

The library was empty except for a senior girl sitting at the main desk studiously filing her fingernails.

"Where's Sister?" Marianne asked.

The girl looked up.

"Hey, they're looking for you!" she exclaimed. "Something has gone wrong with the play, I think. Sister got a phone call about half an hour ago. It got her all upset and she's been tearing around here like a bat out of you-know-where. They're all over at the gym now, I think. Where've you been, anyway?"

"To Confession." Marianne went to the "N's" and took a book off the shelf, glanced at it, shrugged and put it back. She'd better go over to the gym first and see what was up.

Guinevere d'Arblay stood on the gym stage alone, speaking Dorothy's lines and going through Dorothy's movements with exactness and conviction, while Sister Helen, lounging on the stage apron, fed her cues in the traditional speedy monotone of the prompter.

"Are you a good witch or a bad witch?" Sister Helen mumbled.

"Why, I'm not a witch at all," Guinevere cried with a good show of indignation. "I'm a little girl. My name is Dorothy and I come from Kansas."

As Marianne approached, Sister Helen jumped from the apron and hurried toward her, brushing past Sister Anne-

84

Marie, who was sitting on the side bench nervously stitching a tuck in Dorothy's costume.

"Where on earth have you been?" cried Sister Helen. "I have scouting parties all over this campus looking for you."

"I just came from Confession, Sister."

"Oh, splendid. You can pray for us. We need all the help we can get."

"What's wrong?" asked Marianne.

"I sent Jennie home to take a nap. While going up to her bedroom she tripped, fell down a flight of stairs and broke her leg."

Marianne gasped. "Gee, what're you going to do? Can Guinevere take the part?"

"I should say she can. She knows the book cold and the blocking, too. She can even do the mime walk." Sister Helen lowered her voice confidentially. "Sister Anne-Marie thinks there's something untoward about it. Jennie had said some nonsense to Guinevere about breaking her leg."

Marianne looked up at the stage. Guinevere stood now in Jennie Freret's former costume, her arms outstretched like the figure on a crucifix, while Sister Anne-Marie on her knees before her in the manner of a suppliant fussed with the hemline of the costume's pinafore.

"It is sort of weird," Marianne whispered. "What do you think, Sister?"

"At times like this I avoid thinking as much as possible. But in this case I still suspect that coincidence is a more plausible explanation than divine intervention. After all, to everyone but me it's only another school play. With a world as full of misery as this one I'm sure Providence can find better affairs to interfere in. I don't know. I just take it as it comes." She called up to Guinevere, "Shall we go over the songs now, dear?"

Marianne took her place at the piano.

Guinevere knew all the songs and sang them well. She knew all the dance steps and executed them perfectly. After taking her through everything and finding no flaw, Sister Helen escorted her personally back to the convent for lunch and up to the dormitory for a little rest, holding her arm firmly as they mounted the stairs. Then she stopped off at the nuns' chapel to light a candle before the Immaculate Conception. For what intention?

"This is your candle, Holy Mother," she prayed. "I attach no conditions to it. Take it for what you will."

THE CURTAIN was scheduled to rise at eight o'clock. People began assembling in the school yard from seven on, smoking and chattering in the red sunset. At first most of them were parents of performers who, having had to bring their children early, decided it wasn't worth while to return home for less than an hour. After seven-thirty other members of the audience wandered over. There was an air of excitement disproportionate to that warranted by the opening of a small town school play, for all had heard the news of Jennie's inconvenient accident. Was there an understudy? some wondered. No one seemed to know. Giuseppe Verdi Palmisano, who was there with his plump and ever laughing wife, Maria Maddalena, doubted that any provision had been made for one. But he assured anyone who asked him that from all he knew of Sister Helen, the show would go on, if Sister herself had to fill in for Jennie. There was much amusement at this conjecture. Ben Perrier, the impressively rotund mayor of Frenchmen's Bay, boomed forth the opinion that he wouldn't mind seeing that. It would be better than the original. Large men in rumpled seersucker suits laughed with the mayor, while their small ladies in soft pastel voile and organza dresses, clinging lightly to their arms, responded with delicately polite smiles.

As the hour of eight approached couples drifted little by little into the welcomely air-conditioned gym. Confined in this smaller space, the numerous separate conversations became transformed into a muted bedlam of conflicting noises, raising the sense of excitement to a feeling of subdued hysteria.

Backstage the atmosphere was surprisingly calm, for Sister Helen was in charge, and she had warned her cast in advance that she would permit no tears, no fainting and no throwing up. Only the principals on in the early scenes were allowed in the thin corridor which gymnasium architects consider an adequate backstage area. The other players and their costumes were sent to await their entrances in the adjacent fifth grade classroom under Sister Stephanie's stern supervision. Chorus members were confined in other rooms according to the scenes they played in. This grimly organized arrangement was fortunate, for if there had been any relaxation of discipline the news that they were opening with an unknown Dorothy would undoubtedly have brought about the most dreadful confusion and terror. As it was, all anxiety was dutifully suppressed; there were no tears, no fainting and no lost suppers. But underneath the enforced calm everyone was scared, even if truth be told, Sister Helen herself. Guinevere alone remained really calm as she stood at her assigned post against the backstage wall happily humming snatches of melody from her first song.

Sister Anne-Marie, still adjusting the costume designed to fit Jennie Freret, shuddered. Guinevere gave a little yelp.

"What's going on?" Sister Helen demanded sharply.

"I'm sorry, Sister," Guinevere said. "But Sister Anne-Marie stuck a pin in me."

Sister Anne-Marie apologized and after a few more adjustments left the costume to its fate. Sister Helen took her arm and drew her aside.

"You'd better get a hold on yourself, dear," Sister Helen murmured. "You look awful."

"Don't you feel that there's something wrong going on here?" Sister Anne-Marie asked.

"If something is going on, which I am far from ready to admit, I have no idea whether it's right or wrong," said Sister Helen. "I'm withholding judgment until after the show."

She signaled the small group of musicians, who went out front at once, tuning their instruments to the note Marianne sounded on the piano. The audience buzzed into silence as Sister Helen stepped out before the curtain.

"Good evening, ladies and gentlemen. Thank you for joining us tonight. As you may have heard, we have been visited with a small disaster. Because of a most unfortunate accident Miss Jennie Freret cannot be with us, so the part of Dorothy will be played by Miss Guinevere d'Arblay. Thank you."

Over the ripple of polite applause that accompanied Sister Helen's withdrawal behind the curtain, Mayor Perrier's rum-hoarse voice rose.

"D'Arblay? Who's d'Arblay? I don't know any d'Arblay."

Any reply that might have been forthcoming was drowned in the opening of the overture. Marianne and the little combo tried their best to manufacture enthusiasm.

In the makeshift wings of the silly backstage Sister Helen grasped Guinevere's shoulder.

"Do your best, dear," she whispered. "Breathe from the diaphragm and place your voice."

"I will, Sister, don't worry. I'm going to be very good."

And she was. From the instant she skipped onstage with Figaro Palmisano in black tights trotting on all fours behind her she brought life and excitement to what should have been a conventionally pallid amateur production. Even Mrs. Mayor Perrier's shrill exclamation, "Why, it's that dreadful Sylvia Simpson's child!" did not shake her or destroy the enthusiastic response she was getting from the audience.

Sister Helen grasped Sister Anne-Marie around the waist and whirled her about.

"There's your answer, dear, if you insist on having answers," she shouted over the racket of applause coming from the auditorium. "If there has been intervention I swear it's from heaven."

Sister Anne-Marie broke loose.

"I hope you're right, Sister," she whispered. "I hope before God you're right."

She walked swiftly through the fifth grade classroom, brushing past a troop of third and fourth grade munchkins awaiting their entrance.

Sister Stephanie impeded her progress.

"What's happening, Sister?" she demanded.

"I don't know, I don't know," Sister Anne-Marie cried.

"Oh dear," murmured Sister Stephanie. "It sounds rather good from here. The audience is applauding a great deal."

"Yes, yes, I know," said Sister Anne-Marie, grasping the other nun's hand. "Everything's fine, going very well. I'm sure Guinevere is making a great hit."

Sister Stephanie beamed. "Isn't that grand? Almost like a miracle."

The student stage manager peered into the door and beckoned. Sister Stephanie quickly arranged her munchkins in line and headed them into the makeshift wings. "All right now, children. Sing good and loud and don't bump into each other."

Sister Anne-Marie escaped into the muggy school yard. It seemed alive with the calls of night birds and insects and with the presence of something else that Sister Anne-Marie feared to recognize. She shuddered and covered her ears, but she could not shut out the vibrant life that surrounded her. She was afraid, of what she wasn't quite sure, but she could remember being afraid of it when she was a child.

The liveliness of the night was suddenly drowned out by a wave of raucous applause from the gym. That would be the first act curtain. She better go back in to help police intermission. As she opened the door to the fifth grade classroom she shot one quick glance at the bright sky overhead.

"Don't get me wrong, I'm very glad for Sister Helen, but I do wish you'd stay out of it, whatever you are. It's not really any of your business."

II

THE FINAL CURTAIN fell to an uproar that lasted a record fifteen minutes and resulted in an overflowing sellout for the final show Saturday night. The boarders had to be squeezed into the top bleachers to leave room for paying patrons, but despite painful crowding they lustily cheered their compatriot as she showed up all the day students, proving once again the superiority of the community of boarders. Even the proud clique of Spanish students were heard to indulge in an occasional dignified "Olé."

The residents of Dormitory B awaited the star's appearance still rosy with newly rubbed off makeup to set up a great cheer from their curtained beds that set all the other dorms aroar, making the old building shudder under the din. Mother Ignatius in her small private cell at the end of the corridor farthest from the lavatory listened in patient silence, choosing to give the nuns and proctors an equal fifteen minutes to impose order themselves before she made her authority felt.

Everyone had seen the show except the child's own parents, Mother Ignatius brooded, fingering a very generous check which the smitten mayor had presented to her. He had told her when she inquired of him that the wicked "Mrs. Simpson"

90

immediately after surrendering her child to the convent had committed her addicted mother to an expensive nursing home and left town. Mother Ignatius knew better than to pass judgment on another human being, but the contemplation of such waste and emptiness depressed her. She carefully locked the check in a small strongbox which she kept under her bed next to the bottle of port reserved for the relief of the monthly troubles that visited some of the older students and younger nuns. Then, as the noise had subsided, she retired, she hoped, for the night.

It took Sister Helen's best scowls, Sister Stephanie's most brutal threats and as a last resort the possible loss of Saturday movie privileges for two weeks to get the dormitories settled down. Marianne, exhausted but wakeful, lay in bed for a while, but at length rose, despairing of sleep, and sat, as she so often did, at the window staring out onto the splashing bay. The Silver Bullet whistled and clacked its way on up the eastern seaboard, but being a freight train, it carried no dreams with it.

In the quiet dark Marianne tried to sort out the last few days and make some sense of it all. She had the advantage in this case of being a fairly unconcerned observer, which is a rather rare experience for a girl her age. Smiling, she recalled Sister Helen's cool, almost fatalistic opportunism, her conscious refusal to look any gift horse in the mouth, just about what she would have expected of Sister Helen. But she could in no way figure out Sister Anne-Marie's reaction to the whole affair. Sister Anne-Marie had seemed so upset, frightened even, the same nun who had spoken earlier with such scathing assurance about the necessity of belief in the most outrageous miracles. Why, when pressed she had claimed to accept at face value the tale of St. Renatus, a child who had died unbaptized because the local bishop had refused to attend to him until he was done saying Mass. Seven years later the bishop, returned from the wilderness, where he had been doing penance for his negligence, opened Renatus' tomb. The child emerged alive, ready for his christening. In time he grew up to succeed the bishop and both were admitted to the canon of official saints. Marianne could not understand why anyone who could swallow a preposterous tale like that without choking should get upset by a little miracle like Jennie's fall and Guinevere's triumph. Why, that sort of thing happened in the movies all the time. Besides, didn't they all pray, saying a "Hail Mary" every afternoon before rehearsal? What for if not for the success of the play? Well, no one, least of all Sister Anne-Marie, could deny that the prayers had been answered. When there was drought all good Catholics from the Pope on down prayed for rain, but nobody was surprised, much less upset when rain came.

Marianne shrugged and leaned back against the window frame. The adult mind was quite beyond her, in spite of the fact that she was supposed to turn suddenly into an adult in a little more than a week. She closed her eyes tightly, trying to ignore the dormitory night sounds filling the air around her. Dear Lord, she didn't want to spend the rest of her life in a dormitory. She fingered her rosary pensively and wished that her prayers could be answered as readily as Sister Helen's were.

Sister Helen listened from her curtained corner near the door. Her sharp ears detected whispering at the far end of the room. After a minute it stopped and all was quiet again. She took a cylindrical package from under her mattress, slipped it into the wide sleeve of her nightgown and tiptoed down the dorm to Sister Anne-Marie's corner. The younger nun leaped up in alarm when Sister Helen drew back the curtain a little.

"I'm sorry, dear, did I wake you?"

"No," Sister Anne-Marie whispered. "You did startle me, though. I can't sleep, I'm just too upset. But I'm not sure what it is I'm upset about."

"Well, as long as you're up anyway, come on down to the lav and help me celebrate my little triumph."

"To tell you the truth, I don't feel much like celebrating," Sister Anne-Marie hedged. "But I feel even less like lying here brooding. Carry on!"

As they turned toward the door Sister Helen noticed Marianne sitting very still by the window pretending to be oblivious to everything going on in the hope that she in turn would not be observed. But when Sister Helen beckoned imperiously she knew better than to keep up the pretense.

"The convent chapter of Insomniacs Anonymous is meeting in the lavatory. Consider yourself invited, if you can keep your mouth shut."

Sister Helen turned and walked smartly to the door, trailed dubiously by Sister Anne-Marie. Marianne stood a moment, staring after them. Then with a shrug she too went down the hall.

In the lavatory, dimly lit by a shaded night lamp, Marianne was silently handed a Dixie cup which Sister Helen filled with rich dark port from a bottle similar to the one that lay under Mother Ignatius' bed. She took a sip and found it warming and pleasant. She knew that she was enjoying a rare privilege in seeing the nuns without wimple and veil, satisfying every convent child's most compelling question: What color is Sister's hair? Sister Helen's was predictable, severely straight and more or less black, with generous patches of gray. But Sister Anne-Marie's was a rich honey blond, with no suggestion of dark roots, and although cut close to her head, it curled attractively at the nape of her neck. It had not occurred to Marianne that any of the nuns who looked after her spiritual, physical and mental needs might actually be young, much less comely.

Sister Helen raised her Dixie cup in a formal toast.

"Here's to that grand old cliché, the Cinderella story. The promising young understudy takes over for the ailing star and becomes an overnight hit, with a bit of help from the inevitable fairy godmother."

"I don't think that's very funny," Sister Anne-Marie admonished. "This whole business has gotten completely out of hand."

"Oh, come, dear, don't be hard on me," said Sister Helen. "It isn't that often that I end up getting my own way."

"It is exactly what you wished for," said Marianne. "That is a little odd, isn't it?"

"Fortuitous coincidence," Sister Helen replied rather too positively. "That's what most of our miracles probably are."

"Not those miracles recognized by the Infallible Church!" Sister Anne-Marie exclaimed.

Sister Helen shrugged. "Depends on how you look at it, dear. That splendid voice flowing out from the most uninteresting child I've ever worked with is certainly a fortuitous coincidence, but it's miracle enough for me. The Infallible Church probably couldn't care less about the whole business."

"I think we ought to drink to Jennie," said Marianne.

"Right-o!" laughed Sister Helen. "To Jennie, with whom we couldn't have done it." She downed her drink and poured another.

"Really, Sister!" exclaimed Sister Anne-Marie, declining the offer of a refill. Her Dixie cup was still more than half filled. "I think you're heartless. You've scarcely given a thought to that poor injured child. I don't think I care much for miracles that hurt people."

"Nonsense," said Sister Helen. "Jennie asked for it, literally. You heard her yourself. So I suppose she just has to eat her sausage and like it. Speaking of wishes, how's your glimpse of Truth coming along?"

"I really don't know," Sister Anne-Marie replied. "It's hard sometimes knowing whether the glimpse you've had is of Truth or—or something else. If it is Truth, it hurts."

"Ah yes," Sister Helen smiled. "Pilate's problem. It's too bad we don't still have some of those splendid medieval tests for truth. We could throw Guinevere into the bay and see if she floats, or even try Sister Stephanie's cure for visions. If we are going to be plagued with supernatural intervention, it would be helpful if it were a little less ambiguous. One can sympathize with Father Kelly begging for a message."

Marianne leaned back against the sink, relishing the warm, easy feeling the wine gave her. "Follow the Yellow Brick Road," she murmured.

Sister Helen laughed, a bit more loudly than she had meant to. She was feeling the wine a little herself. "Oh yes, that's supposed to be the message, isn't it? It's not such a bad message, really, when you think about it. It has all the virtues of a first-rate oracular pronouncement. It has a nice lilt, sounds good and can mean just about anything you want it to. In fact, it just might be that glimpse of Truth you're so anxious for."

"What about your secret wish, Marianne?" Sister Anne-Marie acknowledged the offer of more wine with a shrug and drank down what she had. "You never let on what you would wish for."

"A one-way ticket," Marianne smiled dreamily. "A one-way ticket anywhere, as far away as possible from dormitories and discipline and Mobile society."

"Bravo!" Sister Helen shouted. "If I weren't fettered with holy poverty I'd buy you one."

"Oh dear," Sister Anne-Marie cried. "What about your vocation? I always thought—"

"That's the trouble." Marianne reached abruptly for the bottle and poured herself a healthy drink. "You always thought, my mother always thought. I wish for once somebody would give me a chance to think for myself. You see that, Sister Helen? It's always like that. Here everybody figures I'm going to take the veil. I'm a good girl, what else could I do? But at home it's a bridal veil they want to fit me for. And me, I don't know that I want any kind of veil at all."

"Well, I've worn both veils," Sister Helen declared, "and I know which one fits more comfortably on me."

Sister Anne-Marie and Marianne exchanged looks over Sister Helen's head. It was an ill-kept secret, for it is hard to keep a secret well in a convent, that Sister Helen had a Past. She had lived a long time in the World, so gossip went, and had been through at least one divorce and perhaps worse before she had escaped into the tranquil life of the convent.

"It's easy for you to talk," said Sister Anne-Marie, who had no Past. "At least you knew what you were giving up."

"Sex?" Sister Helen snickered. "Take my word for it, dear, it's highly overrated. But you do have a point. Do you know what we ought to do while the wishes are still potent? We ought to conjure up a good hot memorable affair for this poor good girl before she takes on either bondage."

"Oh, Sister, really." Sister Anne-Marie put a hand to her mouth.

"There you go again," Marianne retorted with a show of spirit that surprised and delighted Sister Helen. "Making plans for me again. What if I don't want an affair, memorable or not? Damn it—excuse me, Sister, I don't usually swear. I guess it's the wine. I don't usually drink, either. Anyhow, I want to do what I want to do, only, only, I'm not too sure what I want to do."

Her voice trailed off into muddled silence and she hic-coughed.

"Don't worry. You'll find out." Sister Helen caught Sister Anne-Marie by the hand and led her in a ghostly chorus line kick dance, their muslin nightgowns flapping about their feet.

> *"Follow the Yellow Brick Road*
> *Follow the Yellow Brick Road. . . ."*

Giggling, Marianne grabbed the two free hands and they whirled about like the witches in a bad staging of *Macbeth*.

> *"If ever, o ever a whiz there was*
> *The Wizard of Oz is one because—*
> *Because, because, because, because*
> BECAUSE—"

The three collapsed at last, dizzy and shaking with uncontrolled laughter. Sister Helen reached over for the wine bottle, lost her footing and slid down onto the slippery tile floor. Sister Anne-Marie, not much better on her feet, stumbled to her aid. Marianne just sat on the cold tiles panting:

> *"Because of the wonderful things he does. . . ."*

The lavatory door flew open and Sister Stephanie stood incredulous in the doorway.

"What are you doing?" she gasped, although that was obvious. "You-all are going to wake the whole house."

Sister Helen pulled herself up with the help of the washbasin, for her companions were of little use to her.

"Oh dear. I guess we have overdone it a bit."

"I should say you have," Sister Stephanie scolded. "Now you-all get right back to bed before— She's coming!" Sister Stephanie's voice changed from reproval to anxiety. "Mother Ignatius is coming!"

The three women stared at her in distress.

"Here, you. Quick, behind the door," Sister Stephanie whispered. "I'll keep her occupied. You get back into the dorm. And don't make any more noise. Eh, what a mess!"

As the revelers shrank behind the open door Sister Stephanie scooped up the evidence, three paper cups and a nearly empty bottle, and shoved them into the farthest wastebasket, covering them over with paper towels.

When Mother Ignatius burst into the lavatory a few seconds later, she found Sister Stephanie gasping and sobbing and drenching her face with cold water. Mother Ignatius took her firmly by the shoulders.

"Oh dear, Sister. Whatever is wrong?"

"I—I don't know." Sister Stephanie clung to the superior's nightgown. "It was like hell. Everything was on fire. They were chasing me, demons with flaming torches. They set me on fire. Holy saints protect me!"

She sobbed against Mother Ignatius' breast. The sound was remarkably similar to the sound of Sister Helen's laugh. The three behind the door exchanged astonished glances. They had all certainly underestimated Sister Stephanie. Perhaps Sister Helen could find a part for her in the next play.

"Now, now, Sister," Mother Ignatius soothed. "You had a very bad dream, that is all. Come down to my room for a few minutes until you're a little calmer."

Sister Helen peered cautiously around the door as the two

figures faded down the hall. The instant the far door closed behind them she signaled her two companions and, clinging slightly to one another, they hurried fairly quietly back to the dorm.

Twenty minutes later Sister Stephanie also returned to the dorm, having been soothed by Mother Ignatius' gentle sympathy and a sip from Mother Ignatius' private stock. She took a quick check on the drinking partners. They were all safely back in their proper beds, all asleep. Sister Helen was snoring loudly. Marianne half smiled in her sleep, delighted with the discovery that Sister Stephanie's hair was brilliant carrot red.

As she turned back to her own bed, Sister Stephanie remembered the bottle. Cautiously she looked out into the hall. Mother Ignatius' door was closed. Sister Stephanie crept back to the lavatory, retrieved the bottle from the wastebasket and returned just as stealthily to her bed, concealing it in the sleeve of her nightgown.

Sister Stephanie sat on the edge of her bed examining the bottle. There wasn't much left in it so she thought she might as well drink it herself as a reward for her brilliant job of covering for erring sisters. She would have preferred a nice French wine with a château label or perhaps a good cognac, but the port went down nicely all the same. Not having a paper cup, she drank it straight from the bottle. She then hid the bottle in her cupboard. Sometime tomorrow she would smuggle it down to one of the garbage cans.

Sister Stephanie settled down in her bed and drowsily embarked on her favorite nighttime meditation, the contemplation of those ascetic saints who mortified their sinful flesh by scourging it. Sister Stephanie liked to puzzle over what maneuvers they might use to accomplish this physically difficult penance. She did not solve the problem that night. Within ten minutes she also was asleep.

EVERY CONVENT day began officially with the ringing of the electric bell at five-thirty to wake the nuns for six o'clock Mass in the chapel. Every day, including Sunday. Sister Helen roused herself with difficulty. She was dazed and shaky and had a dreadful headache. That showed how much convent life had purified her body as well as her soul. At the height of her worldly career three small cups of port would not have bothered her at all.

Sister Stephanie was in the lavatory when Sister Helen went to wash her face. As the Rule of Silence was in force Sister Stephanie said nothing, but surreptitiously slipped two Alka Seltzers into Sister Helen's hand. Sister Helen acknowledged this act of charity as best she could without risking disobedience to at least the letter of the Rule of Silence.

The second bell rang at half past seven, rousing the girls for eight o'clock Sunday Mass in the church. The nuns, having worshiped and breakfasted, returned to the dorm to get their charges up and herd them into position for the march to church.

As the students assembled two by two in the hall by the main staircase, Brenda Sue sidled up to Guinevere.

"Can I partner you, kid?"

Guinevere looked at her, surprised, for it was no small compliment to be invited to walk with a head girl.

"Sure, I guess so," she murmured.

"You can look on my missal," said Brenda Sue.

Guinevere, who had no missal, was pleased to take up her offer.

"Gee, Brenda Sue," she said, "it's sure nice of you. I didn't think you liked me."

"I've changed my mind about you," Brenda Sue explained. "Since I saw you in that play. I still think you're a fruitcake, but you're a talented fruitcake. And that makes all the difference."

"You'll still give me your grits?"

Brenda Sue shook her head in mock exasperation.

"Sure. You can have my grits and my bread pudding and my stewed tomatoes." She held her belly and made a gagging sound.

99

"Gee, thanks, Brenda Sue," said Guinevere. "Can I do something for you?"

"Yeah, always partner me to church and sing real loud so Sister Helen doesn't pay any mind to me."

"Don't you sing?" Guinevere asked.

"Look, when I sing it sounds like a sea gull with a sore throat. So what do you say I just move my mouth and you sing for the both of us? It'll be a great service to mankind and I'll give you all my garbage."

"OK, it's a deal," said Guinevere.

"Silence," snapped Sister Helen as she took her place at the head of the long double line. But even with her headache and dry mouth Sister Helen observed with satisfaction the evident change in Guinevere's status.

THE BISHOP was present that day for Confirmation. Leonora Palmisano was among the candidates, looking like one of those overdecorated Madonnas one sees in European churches. She was wearing, of course, the Palmisano family Communion dress. This remarkable garment, the work of the family grandma, was ruffled, flounced and embroidered so thoroughly that it could tolerate any number and degree of alterations to fit Palmisanos of all sizes and shapes without betraying tucks and gussets.

Monsignor Fulham debated with himself while assisting at Pontifical High Mass the pros and cons of just casually mentioning to His Grace that one of the convent children was claiming to be blessed with visions. This was, after all, a burden of episcopal proportions. He watched his prelate out of the corner of his eye as he sat, hands ritually folded, listening to the childish voices heavily bolstered by Sister Helen's determined *spinto* and a single clear, pure lyric soprano which he recognized as belonging to the star of last night's show. The Bishop seemed to recognize it too. He had been Monsignor Fulham's guest at the gym and had responded to Guinevere's performance with a few badly hidden tears. Monsignor Fulham smiled a little sadly as he recalled that detail. No, this could not be the Bishop's burden. Sentimental old men ought not to be elevated to the purple, he thought with annoyance. Ah well, it was probably best not to trouble the waters, anyway. He had seen the child transformed overnight from a shy outcast to a minor celebrity. Perhaps, as Sister Anne-Marie had hinted to him backstage, Guinevere's supernatural foster mother had had something to do with that, a hypothesis Monsignor Fulham was in no way advocating. But as things appeared to be working out so well he was more than ever in favor of letting well enough alone, at least unless something more momentous or unusual forced him to reconsider.

> *"Ave Maris Stella*
> *Dei mater alma*
> *Atque semper virgo*
> *Felix coeli porta."*

Monsignor Fulham listened to the ancient chant transformed by the blending of voices, one light and youthful, the other ripe and carefully controlled. Yes, perhaps the Divine Will had already performed its magic trick, and out of the seemingly confused shuffle a woman had emerged with a child and the child with a mother. It was the sort of thing *his* Blessed Mother would have taken pleasure in doing. He noted with a silent sigh as he bowed ritually to the Bishop that His Grace was in tears again.

12

THE MOST IMPORTANT social event of the school year was the Junior-Senior Prom, which took place at the end of May, just prior to graduation. It was an elaborate affair requiring considerable preparation. As soon as *The Wizard* had completed its run, the impatiently waiting juniors who acted as hosts took over the gym. Decoration for the prom was a serious business, for it was the only variable in an inevitable routine. There could be only one place for the celebration, the scene of all convent balls and, for that matter, most other convent activities. There could be only one band hired, the St. Stephen Academy dance band. There were simply no other bands around. Faced with such discouraging uniformity, the juniors, wishing not only to honor the graduating seniors but also to display their own talents, could hardly be expected to settle for balloons and streamers. So it was that the decoration of the gym became one of the most important elements in a convent prom.

To begin with, a theme had to be selected. Abstract decoration, no matter how elaborate, would not do. The gym must be transformed into someplace else, preferably someplace romantic and distant, and (if possible) someplace quite different from the venue of last year's prom.

Theme presented the juniors no problem this year. The imaginary location for the prom had been selected for them by previous use of the gym. This year the prom would be held in the Emerald City of Oz. The town shops were soon bought out of green crepe paper, green construction paper, green poster paint and green net. Then one of the wealthier juniors had an inspiration. Why not make the Emerald City sparkle with the latest item on the market, green aluminum foil wrapping paper? That really demolished the junior class budget, but none could deny that the effect was striking.

Sister Anne-Marie, who was supposed to be supervising the decorating efforts, stood by the gym door a few days before the event, her arms folded, watching this extraordinary after-school activity. While girls who were decent in art painted a backdrop of emerald streets lined with emerald houses or labored at the construction of a huge pâpier-maché Wizard sitting on an elaborate emerald plywood throne, their less talented but equally eager classmates made emerald crepe paper rosettes or covered Chinese lanterns with emerald cellophane. Their eagerness and happy expectation depressed Sister Anne-Marie, for she had seen it all so many times and knew what it would be like when the prom was over and they all came back to clean up the debris in the morning. Some would still be glowing from the triumph of their big night, others would be bravely hiding disappointment over an unpleasant or just a dull evening. The backdrop would be torn, the rosettes trampled, and some girl was sure to cut her hand on a piece of glass.

Sister Anne-Marie turned away and took the stairs up to the second floor of the new building. She had thought of sitting in on Guinevere's voice lesson, but as she approached the music room and caught the "me-he-wa-ha-me" of those endless chromatic scales she changed her mind. She couldn't stand a half hour of me-he-wa-ha-me. She just wasn't in the mood. Her period was due, and she was suffering from that premenstrual depression which made everything she observed appear either futile or tedious.

103

From one of the practice rooms along the hall came a sound that was neither futile nor tedious, but to Sister Anne-Marie's ears extraordinarily disturbing. She softly opened the door and went in. Marianne Brandon was playing something on the piano, something unfamiliar to Sister Anne-Marie. It was romantic in style, violently agitated in tone to the point of hysteria. And Marianne was attacking the piano as though she meant to destroy it. Sister Anne-Marie sat on a chair by the wall listening to this performance, fascinated and slightly terrified. There was a communication going on here between composer and performer that she had not before witnessed. It was as though Marianne were no longer doing the playing herself but had become one with the passion trapped in the music, and there was in it an undertone of madness. Marianne concluded this demonic waltz with a flourish and a crashing chord.

"What on earth was that?" Sister Anne-Marie gasped.

"Schumann's *Carnaval*. That finale is supposed to be David marching against the Philistines. Isn't that rare? I always play Schumann when I'm in a dither. The nerves in his music always seem to calm my own nerves. I suppose that's more therapy than art, but it works." Marianne turned on the piano bench, wiped her sweating face with a handkerchief and pushed back her hair. "He had a rough life, Schumann did. He went out of his mind and died in a madhouse. He said the angels were dictating music to him. I don't know, maybe they were." She looked hard at Sister Anne-Marie. "Where do you draw the line between the madman and the saint?"

"I'm sure I don't know," Sister Anne-Marie snapped. She did wish people would stop bringing up things like that. She did not want to think about them, not now when everything had settled down. Just the thought of saints and even of angels getting involved in the affairs of men made her nervous. She quickly changed the subject.

"What's got you in a dither? Surely you're not worrying about exams?"

"I just found out what my graduation gift is—a genuine

old-fashioned Mobile society debut. It'll bankrupt my poor daddy, but it will get me into the market for eligible bachelors."

"Oh well," said Sister Anne-Marie. "If it's already settled you may as well make the best of it. I always thought it would be nice to have a debut. Of course, one way out of it would be to announce unequivocally your intention to enter the novitiate."

This time it was Marianne's turn to wince. She did wish Sister Anne-Marie would quit shoving the novitiate down her throat.

"You don't know my mother," she countered. "And if the convent thing doesn't work out I would never hear the end of it. On days like this I could almost wish for that affair of Sister Helen's, only it might come true." She laughed a little harshly. "Good heavens, who could I have an affair with? Even my prom date is all but celibate." She slammed her hands down hard on the keyboard in front of her, filling the little practice room with the dissonance of frustration.

"Gee, Sister, don't you ever feel trapped?"

Sister Anne-Marie rose quickly. "Of course not," she snapped. "I just can't understand you girls anymore. You act like boys and talk like, like sluts. I think the best thing you can do is make up your mind once and for all what you intend to do with the gift of life God has granted you, and then stick with it. If you don't settle down soon you're going to fall into sin and be lost. Oh dear. I just wouldn't have thought it of you."

Agitated, she crossed to the window and looked out.

"Good heavens," she cried. "What's going on down there?"

Marianne joined her, peering over her shoulder down onto the school yard. A group of younger boarders were crowding excitedly around a large maroon Cadillac limousine stopped in the yard. A uniformed chauffeur got out of the driver's seat, pushed through the gaping children and opened the rear door. Out stepped a strikingly beautiful young woman, richly and fashionably dressed. Despite the heat she was wearing a pale fur stole of whole pelts with pretty little dead faces draped over her shoulder. Her face was tanned to a warm gold, which contrasted beautifully with her carefully dressed shining blond hair. She looked for a long second at the group of dirty children staring openmouthed at her as at the sudden apparition of a fairy tale princess. She honored them with a slow, close-mouthed smile, reached into the alligator handbag on her arm and began passing around amongst them shiny dimes and quarters. Sister Anne-Marie ran down the steps and out to the yard, with Marianne panting behind her.

"Go on with you," she shouted to the children pushing and grasping for the coins. "Get about your business, now!" She raised her hand threateningly and the children fled.

"Good afternoon, I'm Sister Anne-Marie," she said, trying to collect her dignity. She noticed at close range that the woman was not as young as she had seemed at first and that to a great extent her beauty was applied with a brush.

"How do you do?" The woman extended a bronze-colored hand decorated with a large diamond and crimson fingertips. "I'm Sylvia Simpson."

She said the name in a positive manner, obviously expecting Sister Anne-Marie to recognize it. She did not. The embarrassing silence in which she searched her mind desperately for some reference to "Simpson" was broken by Marianne's exclamation: "Oh, Guinevere's mother."

"My, what a pleasant surprise," Sister Anne-Marie cried at once. "I don't believe she's expecting you. She's having a music lesson now. I'll go—"

"I'd like to see the mother superior first, if that's possible," Sylvia Simpson interrupted, a sudden brief look of anxiety escaping from under her makeup.

"Yes, of course," murmured Sister Anne-Marie. "I'm sure Mother Ignatius will be delighted to see you. Come with me, please."

They walked together through the basement and up the main staircase. Sister Anne-Marie did not speak. She felt bewildered and uncomfortable in the company of this creature from the alien world outside the convent. From every dim corner she seemed to see pairs of avaricious little eyes peering.

Mother Ignatius rose as they entered, smiling graciously, as if the intruder were a familiar and invited guest. Sister Anne-Marie skirted the problem of the embarrassing surname by simply introducing the stranger as Guinevere's mother and fled, relieved, back to the pure unpainted sunshine of the school yard.

"Well," Mother Ignatius said, facing her guest across the desk, her hands folded like a Gothic church roof so that the fingertips just touched. "It's too bad you weren't here last week. Your daughter took over the lead in the school play and had quite a triumph."

"Really? I didn't know she could do anything like that."

"Oh yes, she's very talented," said Mother Ignatius. "You've been away, I take it?"

"Yes. Taking the cure, so to speak. I had a sort of a nervous breakdown. Tried to do myself in. Very foolish."

"You're better now?" Mother Ignatius prodded.

"Oh yes. I'm all right now. I'm off the sauce, at least."

Mother Ignatius looked blank.

"The sauce?"

"I've quit drinking."

"Oh, I see," said Mother Ignatius. "I'm very glad to hear that."

Sylvia Simpson fumbled nervously in her alligator bag.

"It's helped a lot knowing that little Guinevere was safe with you. I could be sure you would be nice to her."

"It's no chore being nice to Guinevere," said Mother Ignatius. "She's a very well-behaved and likable child."

"She is, isn't she? Much too good for me."

The woman took from her bag an engraved gold box from which she partially drew out a brown-tipped cigarette. She made a motion as though to offer the box to Mother Ignatius, but, thinking better of it, took the cigarette herself, putting the brown tip in her mouth. Then she looked expectantly at the superior and the desk, but apparently not seeing what she wanted, she began searching through her bag.

"You've returned to Frenchmen's Bay?" asked Mother Ignatius.

Sylvia Simpson shook her head. She had by now succeeded in extracting from her bag an engraved gold lighter which she had to press three or four times before producing a flame. She lit her cigarette, drew in hard on it, held her breath for a second and then blew out a puff of strong-smelling smoke.

"Not if I can help it," she said. "This place is bad news for me. I'm going right back where I came from as soon as possible."

"And where is that?" asked Mother Ignatius.

"Nassau."

"Oh yes. That's in the Bahamas, isn't it?" Mother Ignatius murmured. "How nice for Guinevere."

There was a long pause. Sylvia smoked hard on her cigarette.

"You've never been there, have you, Mother?" she said at last.

"No, I can't say that I have."

"Take my word for it, it's no proper place for a child, not for a nice little girl like Guinevere. It's all—well, night life, you know—and like that." She leaned forward, extending the cigarette, now burdened with a cylinder of gray ash, gingerly in front of her. She was looking for something again. Mother Ignatius took from her desk drawer a metal can filled with paper clips and placed the lid upside down in front of her guest. The two women exchanged a look of mutual understanding as Sylvia deftly flicked the ash into the lid.

"I don't expect you to approve of my way of life, but—"

"But there is no place in it for a half-grown child," Mother Ignatius snapped.

Sylvia lowered her eyes and puffed in silent intensity on her cigarette. There was another of those nasty little pauses.

"The school term ends in ten days," Mother Ignatius said

quietly. "We do not run a summer session. Many of the sisters go away for study and retreats. There are no children here all summer."

A slow, bitter smile spread across the other woman's face.

"So you don't want her either." She ground the cigarette savagely against the tin lid and arranged her handbag as though ready to depart. "Never mind, then. I can always ship her off to one of those country club summer camps in the New England mountains."

"That sounds very nice," said Mother Ignatius.

Sylvia Simpson gave one low snort.

"You've never been there either, I see. I spent all my summers in places like that when I was growing up. They're not at all nice, not what you mean by nice. Junior Nassau, that's what they are. They take nice kids like Guinevere and turn them into—people like me."

Mother Ignatius stared at her fingers and spoke slowly.

"It's not really a matter of our not wanting her. We're all very fond of her. She's a dear child and no trouble to anyone. The question is whether she would want to stay here all summer with the other children gone. Have you asked her about it?"

Sylvia shook her head.

"I haven't seen her yet. I wanted to talk to you first." She leaned forward with a show of earnestness. "You have no idea what it has meant to me knowing she was here, being looked after by people like you. You may not believe it, but I really do want her to be happy."

"Then first of all you must ask her what she wants. It is only after her happiness is considered that we can think of deciding what is best for her."

Sylvia rose. "All right, Mother. I'll talk it over with her, man to man, so to speak. And whatever she really wants, that's what I'll do."

Mother Ignatius also rose. She was deeply disturbed by this interview, more than her guest could possibly realize. For she knew one very powerful reason why it might be best for

109

Guinevere to be anywhere but the convent left on her own all summer, free to spend as much time as she pleased at the Shrine. Mother Ignatius knew that she had a duty to inform the child's mother of this particular problem.

"Just a moment, please," she called abruptly.

Sylvia Simpson turned, her hand on the doorknob.

"Is something wrong?"

"Oh no, no," Mother Ignatius cried, suddenly confused and uncertain. How could she just out and tell this woman? "It—it's just that . . . Well, we've observed that Guinevere has—has a very vivid imagination."

"Really?" The other woman seemed genuinely surprised. "That goes to show how well I know my own child. I never knew her to show any imagination at all."

There was another awkward silence. Mother Ignatius opened her mouth, then closed it again.

"What is the matter?" Sylvia demanded, showing some anxiety. "Is she in some kind of trouble?"

"Oh no, of course not!" Mother Ignatius exclaimed. "She's the best-behaved child in the school. It's just that, you see, she —she's well, uh, very devoted to the Blessed Mother."

"Oh," the other laughed in relief, failing to mark the superior's discomfiture. "I suppose she has to have some kind of mother, hasn't she?" With that she swept out of the office. Mother Ignatius half rose, then sat down heavily, covering her face with her hands, hot with shame for her cowardice and trembling in sudden fear. She could not but feel that she had been prevented from saying what she meant to.

SISTER ANNE-MARIE, who was waiting on a bench near the parked limousine, guarding against a repetition of the earlier, slightly Dickensian scene, escorted Sylvia to the music room. As they walked down the hall they could hear a delicate, clear voice coming from the room at the end of the hall:

"*Panis angelicus, fit panis Dominum,*
Dat panis coelitus, figuris terminum."

110

The held note wavered and then faded ignominiously.

"No, dear." Sister Helen's voice could be heard through the closed door. "That won't do. You're not breathing from the diaphragm. Shall we try it again?"

Sister Anne-Marie rapped sharply at the door. There was a pause, then the door slowly opened.

"Yes?" Sister Helen inquired coolly.

"Sylvia!" Guinevere squealed as she caught sight of the visitor. Mother and daughter stumbled sentimentally into each other's arms. They drew back and looked at each other with comically similar expressions of inquiry followed by a unison exclamation:

"Gee, you look great!"

After another embrace seasoned with tearful laughter, Guinevere recovered her composure enough to make the superfluous introduction.

"Sister Helen, this is my mother."

Sister Helen took the woman's hand warmly. "I'm delighted to meet you," she said. "We have so enjoyed having your daughter amongst us."

"Sister Helen's teaching me to sing," Guinevere said proudly.

"From what I heard just now, I think she must have a very easy job."

Guinevere shook her head. "I don't breathe right. But I'm learning."

"So you are, and very well," said Sister Helen. "Lesson's over for today. You run along now and have a nice visit."

"Thanks, Sister." Guinevere caught her mother by the hand and began pulling her down the hall. "Come on, Sylvia, I want to show you the Shrine."

The little garden that surrounded the Shrine was cool and delicately fragrant with blooming roses. Sylvia examined the blue-robed statue a few minutes before joining Guinevere on a bench.

"You like her, don't you?" she said as much for a conversation opener as anything else.

111

Guinevere's eyes shone. "Oh yes. We're great friends."

"Isn't that sweet?" Sylvia smiled benevolently.

Guinevere would have elaborated had she not been prevented by Sylvia's anxiety to get right into the problem of the summer.

"You are happy here, honey?" she asked.

"Oh yes!" Guinevere exclaimed. "It's great here. They give you lots to eat. Monsignor Fulham's teaching me the Catechism so I can make my First Communion. And I was Dorothy in *The Wizard of Oz*, and everybody clapped and made a big fuss. You should have seen me."

"I wish I had seen you," Sylvia murmured, putting her arm around Guinevere's shoulders. "I've been away all spring, just trying to get straightened out. At least I'm off the sauce now."

"Oh, that's wonderful. I'm so glad." Guinevere returned her gesture with an ebullient hug, then asked hesitantly, "What about Tony?"

"I haven't laid eyes on that miserable parasite since he walked out, thank God. I'm well rid of him, too. I have a new boyfriend. Don't worry, he's no Tony. He's a true gentleman. He sends fresh flowers to my room every day and orders dinner in perfect French." She laughed lightly. "Who knows, sweetheart, maybe I'm really in love at last. Maybe I'll come home someday with a daddy for you worthy of the name."

"That'd be swell." Had she been less involved with herself Sylvia might have noticed the slightly patronizing tone in her daughter's voice. "Are you going back to him now?"

"Yes. As soon as I can get some business straightened out here. He's in Nassau. That's somewhere down in the south sea." She waved her hand vaguely in the direction of the bay, as she wasn't quite sure where it was herself. "You can come along, too, if you want, though it's not much of a place for kids. Or you can stay here if you'd rather."

"Oh no," Guinevere said. "I don't think I can stay here. They close the school all summer."

"The mother superior says you can stay here if you want."

Guinevere stared at her, incredulous. "Could I? Could I really?"

Sylvia nodded, rather taken aback by the ease of her victory. "You can do whatever you want, sweetheart."

"Oh, thank you, thank you." Guinevere threw her arms around her mother's neck and kissed her. She leaped up suddenly and ran to the foot of the statue.

"Do you hear? Do you hear that?" she shouted at it. "I'm going to stay here with you all summer. Just what I wished. I'm going to be with you always. Always!"

Sylvia rose abruptly from her seat, alarmed at first by this outburst, but ready on second thought to attribute it to the devotion mentioned by Mother Ignatius. After all, now she could go back to Nassau with a free conscience, knowing that her child was happy. And she had certainly never seen Guinevere happier. Her eyes were shining as she turned back from the Shrine in a way Sylvia had never known them to before. Well, she wasn't going to object. Let everyone find happiness where she could.

While Sylvia went to confer with Mother Ignatius on the arrangements for the summer, Guinevere joined the other boarders around the lunch cart.

"Is that your mother?" asked Brenda Sue Foote, staring as though hypnotized at the grand figure floating up the staircase.

Guinevere nodded proudly. "Isn't she beautiful?"

Brenda Sue whispered to the girl next to her, "Did you see that rock on her finger? It must have weighed four carats!" To Guinevere she said almost reproachfully, "You never told me you were rich."

"Oh." Guinevere seemed surprised. "I didn't know it was important. But I've got real news, Brenda Sue, wonderful news. They're going to let me stay here all summer. When the rest of you have to go, I'm going to stay right here. Isn't that terrif?"

Brenda Sue stared at her for a long minute. "Yeah," she said at last in a flat voice. "That's great, just great." She turned and walked away with the girl next to her, muttering:

"What can you do with a kid like that? Maybe she's rich and maybe she's talented, but why for corn's sake does she have to be such a fruitcake?"

13

AT THE END of May the senior class graduated with modest ceremony, all in white like novices making their first vows, the black cap and gown like the black habit being reserved for more serious commencements. By special request of the graduates Guinevere d'Arblay sang the "Alma Mater," a bit of hopelessly sentimental doggerel inappropriately set to Parry's "Jerusalem." Sister Helen reluctantly tolerated this exploitation of her protégé, but firmly put her foot down at an encore of "Over the Rainbow" as just too much sentimentality splashed over an already overly sentimental ritual.

She stood on the rear veranda with Sister Anne-Marie that evening watching the last of the senior boarders load up their parents' cars and depart.

"You met Marianne's parents," Sister Anne-Marie remarked.

"Just what you'd expect. Daddy's a meek and quiet southern gentleman; Mother runs the show. Marianne will have to be a lot stronger than she appears to be to get the better of that one without some outside help."

"Don't talk about outside help," Sister Anne-Marie said hastily.

Sister Helen laughed. "Don't worry, dear. I didn't wish it."

"Barring, God forbid, outside help, what do you think will happen to Marianne?" asked Sister Anne-Marie.

"The inevitable. She'll get bored or disgusted and marry the first good-looking fellow who asks her. You did it the easy way, straight from school to the novitiate. The pressure of the world is hard to resist when everyone else is pairing off and getting rings and buying china."

"Nothing is too hard to resist if you have a true vocation," Sister Anne-Marie said firmly. "You dedicate your life to God and that's that."

Sister Helen smiled slightly. "I wouldn't know about that, dear. I wasn't blessed with a vocation. I'm here because this way of life suits me. If my life is pleasing to God as well, so much the better."

The last trunk-laden car pulled out of the convent driveway. Sister Helen turned back to the door leading into the cool main hall.

"Well, that's that until September. I wonder if the little devils realize that we are as glad to be rid of them as they are to be gone. Nobody here but us chickens."

She did a sedate soft shoe turn.

"And Guinevere," Sister Anne-Marie reminded her. "By the way, where is Guinevere?"

Sister Helen stopped her shuffle, one hand on the worn latch.

"She was down in the yard a while ago saying good-bye to everyone quite as if she were the hostess breaking up a garden party. I have no idea where she is now."

The eyes of both women went at once toward the dirt path leading to the Shrine. The sound of a clear young voice chanting some uninspired children's hymn heralded Guinevere's approach. An instant later she came in sight, leading Sister Clementine by the hand, tempering her energy in deference to the old nun's arthritis. She waved smiling brightly to the sisters on the veranda.

"Oh, dear Lord," whispered Sister Anne-Marie. "Don't tell me that's going to start again."

116

"To tell you the truth," said Sister Helen, "I don't think it ever stopped. Apparently Sister Clementine was right, when Our Blessed Mother really wants something, she manages to get it one way or another." She turned abruptly and went into the convent.

In those days the highway followed the coast, crossing the bay on a rickety three-mile bridge where leather-skinned old women and nearly naked boys fished from the rails. The road widened and divided on the far side of the bay to allow a palm-lined, landscaped island to flourish in its center. Marianne Brandon sat in the back seat of her parents' sleek hardtop convertible, holding her hair against the strong wind blowing back from the open front windows and staring blankly at the beautiful seascape hurrying by. In the front passenger seat her mother talked nonstop, about the graduation, the other girls, their parents, the dullness of convent life compared with the delights of the Mobile season, and worst of all, plans for the future. Marianne sat quiet with her own thoughts, contributing the occasional obligatory "Yes'm" without paying any attention to what was being said. She was thinking of the railroad trestle that had crossed the bay parallel to the highway bridge. The L&N tracks she knew followed the same coast a couple of miles north of the beach. The Crescent Limited out of New Orleans would pass through Mobile on its way north around midnight. She would be able to hear it from her house every night when it passed.

14

AFTER THE EXODUS of the boarders the now nearly deserted convent settled down into a comfortable routine. The cool of the morning was the time for the more strenuous labor of cleaning out the residue of the school year from classrooms, dorms and grounds. The heat of the day was spent in quiet activity, reading and studying in the library, taking tedious inventories of textbooks and supplies. Guinevere, accustomed to making herself inconspicuous, fitted easily into the routine. She was a willing worker, joining unbidden into any activity she came across. Soon she was all but taken for granted, as much a part of the community as any of the sisters. Even Sister Anne-Marie began to relax a little and stop watching her with such intensity. On hot afternoons before the inevitable late afternoon thundershower relieved the humidity a little, while the rest of the community was at study or siesta, the child walked alone down the cinder path to the Shrine, weeding the borders as she went. She was always back in the annex waiting when Sister Helen lumbered over, yawning, for a music lesson. No one seemed to be paying much attention to what was going on, except Sister Clementine, who smiled and kept her peace. She did, however, take pains to advise her

118

Blessed Mother that it was no doubt best to do nothing to call attention to her continued presence—for the sake of the camellias. Perhaps the others had not so much forgotten about her presence as just given in to it. It was a problem best solved sometime later.

The closing of school also marked the unofficial start of the summer season in the town, its major industry. The natives sighed, battened their hatches and raised their prices in honor of the summer people who now invaded Frenchmen's Bay in such numbers that the population trebled. The large beachfront houses of wealthy New Orleanians were opened and aired in anticipation of the return of their seasonal tenants seeking the elusive Gulf breeze. The little steam-driven commuter train that wheezed its way daily from Pascagoula to Canal Street and back again doubled its length from three to six cars, crowding the established poker game of the regulars who commuted year round.

Summer business was healthy at the Freret Stables, situated on an eighty-acre estate, "Liveoaks," five miles north of Frenchmen's Bay. The landscaping there was as conventional as the name, most of the land being used for grazing; smooth, faceless meadows peppered occasionally with moss-draped gnarled oak trees, like trolls' umbrellas. The house was a patioed rambling white ranch type modeled on one featured in *House and Garden,* with an imitation ante-bellum pillared veranda slapped on the front like a movie set façade. Inside it was furnished in showroom Early American made ludicrous by an occasional genuine antiquity. The antiques were the fruits of frequent ventures into the back country amongst the fishing shacks along the bayous and the sharecroppers' cabins on the inland plantations. The walnut washstand topped with a fine slab of brown marble that stood against the paneled kitchen wall had stood before in the single room of an old farmer's cabin covered with five coats of sickening green paint. He had been happy to sell it for ten dollars, unaware of what a little paint remover and linseed oil could do for it.

Business here was not quite as usual. Jennie, hot and bored, hobbled down from her room, making a face at the freshly squeezed orange juice waiting for her on the polished maple kitchen table. Her mother had read somewhere that there was no substitute for freshly squeezed orange juice and so refused to have anything to do with canned or the new frozen juice. Jennie hated freshly squeezed orange juice, for it was filled with pulp and small seeds. She downed it in one shuddering gulp, anxious to get the ordeal over with, and settled down to the more palatable bowl of shredded wheat.

"Good morning, dear," her mother said.

"Morning, Mom," Jennie muttered. "My cast itches."

Jennie's mother sighed. This was turning into the longest summer she could remember. She felt sorry for Jennie, of course; it was hard on an active child being burdened with a cumbersome cast. But it was also a terrible strain on the adults trying to be patient and keep her occupied. As Jennie's mother had been reading a book on positive thinking, she attempted to apply the precepts to her present problem.

"And what are you planning to do today?" she asked brightly.

Jennie shrugged off the positive approach. "Sit and stare at the wall, I guess. It's no fun fooling around the horses when I can't ride, and the only things on TV are *Industry on Parade* and civil defense junk. You got any ideas?"

"Why don't you have some of your friends over?"

"Church kids?" Jennie snorted contempt. "I'd sooner look at the wall."

"And what's wrong with the young people at church?" her mother demanded.

"Oh, they're either babies that play with dolls or boring brains that keep jabbering in long words about things I don't understand or knotheads that just sit around and giggle about boys. I haven't got a friend in the bunch."

"You have friends from school, don't you?"

"Oh yeah. But you wouldn't have my only real friends in the house."

"What kind of thing is that to say?" her mother responded

120

indignantly, turning from the sink with a cup of coffee in her hand. Why wouldn't I want your friends in the house?"

"'Cause one's a dago and the other's a witch."

"Jennifer! That's not nice and you know it. We say an Italian."

"Daddy says dago." Jennie spooned a great mound of strawberry-flavored powder purported to be loaded with vitamins into her milk and stirred vigorously.

"You are not to say it, all the same. And not even your daddy says that other word, at least not when there are ladies present." Jennie's mother cleared the table, dumping the juice glass and cereal bowl into the suds-topped dishpan. "I honestly don't know where you pick up the language you use."

Jennie giggled. "Not bitch, Mom. Witch."

"Well, that's not a very nice thing to say about a friend," her mother said.

"Oh, but it's true, Mom. How do you think I broke my leg?"

"You fell down the steps."

"Uh-uh. She put a spell on me and made me fall." Jennie was enjoying herself. Shocking her mother was one of her favorite pastimes. "She did it as a special favor to me. I told her I wanted to break my leg so I wouldn't have to make a fool of myself in that show. She said hocus-pocus in the right places and whee! down I went. It's just great having a witch for a best friend."

"Nonsense," her mother snapped.

"Have it your way," Jennie laughed. She gathered her crutches and hobbled out onto the patio. Her mother looked after her, puzzled. It wasn't like Jennie, that sort of talk. Maybe she was being left too much to herself. According to an article in *Good Housekeeping*, children left too much to themselves tend to invent private fantasy worlds and even to believe in them. That certainly sounded sinister. After a moment of thought Jennie's mother dried her hands and lifted the receiver of the kitchen telephone.

121

"Number, please," a nasal voice chanted in her ear.

"The convent, please. I think it's 208-J."

THE FRERETS' well-used station wagon pulled into the empty convent yard less than an hour later. Guinevere was waiting in the shade of the veranda; Sister Helen was with her. Jennie's mother winced at the sight of the girl, for in all that heat she was dressed in the regulation convent gym suit, a pale blue horror of modesty, complete with bloomers and a skirt, like a Victorian bathing dress. Poor dear child, Jennie's mother thought. Loaded with money and she didn't even have proper summer clothes.

"I'll have her back by four," she told Sister Helen.

"That will be fine," said Sister Helen. "Have a good time, dear."

The wagon drove off, turning back from the beach, through the town and across the tracks.

"It must be lonely at the convent all by yourself," Jennie's mother said.

"Oh, I'm not by myself. Most of the sisters are there, and Tootsie comes over a lot. It's terrif being the only kid. I can do what I please most of the time, and I get all the food I want."

The wagon pulled up in front of a rambling frame house with a large vegetable garden in the rear.

Tootsie flew out of the house, sending the chickens that roamed the yard into fluttering retreat. She was folllowed by her plump mother, panting to keep up. The Italian child was really rather attractive, Jennie's mother had to admit as she met them at the gate. Her long black hair had been arranged in shoulder-length finger curls and then carefully gathered into bunches on either side of her head. Rather old-fashioned, but on Tootsie it looked good. And she was dressed most sensibly in shorts and a midriff blouse of some coarse, cool-looking material printed in a cheery flower pattern. The pattern looked familiar to Jennie's mother, but it wasn't till quite a while later that she identified it as feed sacks.

122

Tootsie's mother placed a large warm pan in Jennie's mother's hands.

"Deep dish blackberry pie," she explained. "The children picked the berries themselves."

It was Jennie's mother's first inclination to politely refuse the gift, which people like the Palmisanos could scarcely afford, but the odor of warm pastry and cinnamon coming from the dish prevented her. Well, if the children had picked the berries. She accepted the pie with thanks, forgetting for a while her *Ladies' Home Journal* Foolproof Ten-Day Wonder Diet.

JENNIE WAS waiting on the pillared front porch, hopping up and down on her crutches. Her mother stood back and watched with amusement and a little nostalgia the ritual of squealing embraces as the friends were reunited. She even supplied a pen for the autographing of the cast. Then, well satisfied with her morning's work, she retired into the cool solitude of the house, freed for a while at least from the often wearisome duties of motherhood to read the latest historical novel and make a few phone calls in preparation for the annual Sunday School picnic.

Jennie escorted her guests to her favorite sitting and thinking place on a grassy hill overlooking the pasture and stable. They sat in the shade of a huge old liveoak tree, its venerable branches draped in delicate gray lace veils of Spanish moss as if it were in mourning for a South long dead and only dimly commemorated in squat, thin-pillared front porches.

"How're you doing, Jennie?" Guinevere asked a little hesitantly.

"Oh, I'm doing great!" Jennie exclaimed. "You really fixed me up. I heard you were real good in the play."

"Oh, she was," Tootsie cried. "Everyone says she's as good as Judy Garland. Did the Blessed Mother really make you break your leg? Sister said you fell down the steps."

Jennie shook her head. "Something made me fall down the steps. It was real queer. Mom sent me upstairs to take a rest. It seemed kind of dim in the house, like night was coming. I was thinking about the Yellow Brick Road, and then I saw it. I guess it was really the stair carpet, but it looked like yellow bricks and it sparkled. And I saw something, somebody, I don't know, standing at the top of the steps. It was like a shadow, but solid—a ghost or, or an angel. I was scared but I kept walking toward it up the Yellow Brick Road. I don't think it touched me, but it held up its arms and—I guess I stepped back, and down I went."

"Did it hurt a lot?" Tootsie asked, wide-eyed.

"No. That's another funny thing. When I woke up the doctor was here and all, and he kept asking me if I was in pain. But I wasn't. The doctor told Mom I was in shock." She giggled. "It never started hurting, so I guess I'm still in shock. Of course I complain a lot because I can make them give in to me if I work on their sympathy. That's how I got you two over here today. It's really been terrif. Look, I got all kinds of nice things at the hospital, got out of school early, can't do my chores and can't swim. Thanks just loads."

"Don't you like to swim?" asked Tootsie, more astonished by this revelation than by Jennie's experience on the stairs. Supernatural wonders she took as a matter of course.

"Swimming?" Jennie made a face. "Yuck. I hate it. It's worse than school. Me, I have to do it right. I can't just paddle around like other kids. I have to swim properly."

"Gee, I can't swim at all," said Guinevere. "It looks like fun watching."

"It's easy," said Tootsie. "I can show you. I learned off Manny year before last. We swim from the convent pier a lot."

"Yeah, but you-all don't swim right," said Jennie. She had gathered a small pile of white clover blossoms around her and now began weaving them into a chain. "I've got to do everything right, by the book. My mom believes in the book. When I was a real little kid, maybe three or four, she read in a book or article or something how to teach real little kids to swim. And she did it all with me, step by step, and I hated every hour of it. I had to learn to swim and learn the right way 'cause they wouldn't let me out of the pool until I did it right.

Oh, I'm a real good swimmer, sure. I win races and all that stuff. But not this summer." Jennie laughed. She took the clover wreath she had made and laid it like a crown on Guinevere's head. "This summer I can't swim at all 'cause I've got a broken leg, thanks to my best friend, the witch."

The other two girls looked at her, startled.

"What do you mean by that?" Tootsie cried.

"Oh, she's not a wicked witch, of course," said Jennie. "She's a good witch. A very good witch."

"But I'm not a witch at all," Guinevere wailed. "I'm a little girl. My name is Dorothy—I mean my name is Guinevere." She subsided in confusion, but then lashed out with sudden vehemence. "What's the big idea calling me a witch?"

"I don't mean anything bad," said Jennie. "Honest, Gwen. It's just that you make things happen, and that's kind of spooky. But the things you make happen are the things people want to happen, so you must be a good witch."

"She doesn't make things happen," Tootsie protested. "It's the Blessed Mother that makes things happen."

"That's OK for you," said Jennie. "You're a Catholic. I'm a Presbyterian and we don't have a Blessed Mother and saints and things. We only have stuff that's in the Bible."

"Oh dear," said Tootsie. "Your church must be awfully dull. Anyhow, the Blessed Mother is in the Bible."

"Only as a mother," said Jennie. "She's not blessed and she doesn't get a capital letter. But there are witches in the Bible. I asked Reverend Moore when he visited me in the hospital and he said there were, but he thought they were always bad. I don't know. There's bad angels in the Bible and a holy ghost, so I don't see why there can't be good witches."

"I like the Blessed Mother better," said Tootsie, complacent in her colorful Catholicism. "Does she do everything you ask her to, Gwen?"

"Oh, I never ask her to do anything," said Guinevere. "I just talk to her, you know, about what's going on and what people say and stuff like that. She just listens and don't say much at all, except sometimes when she asks me questions or explains things to me."

Jennie wiped her face, for the heat was intense, more like August than June, and for once there was no cooling breeze blowing up from the bay.

"What if you told her I was thirsty and wanted a pitcher of cold lemonade?"

"Oh, Jennie." Tootsie was shocked. "You mustn't ask for things like that. You're supposed to ask for important things."

It was Guinevere's turn to be shocked.

"I think food's very important," she said sternly.

"Did you ever ask for food?" Jennie inquired.

"Not right out," said Guinevere. "But once I did tell her I was hungry sometimes. The next morning Brenda Sue started giving me her grits."

"Well, I do wish you'd try for some lemonade now."

Tootsie looked doubtful. "She might not like it."

"She wouldn't do anything to us if she got mad, would she?" Jennie asked uncertainly. "There's a story they tell us in Sunday School about some kids who were teasing a funny-looking old prophet. Bears came and ate them all up."

Tootsie laughed. "Oh, she wouldn't do nothing like that. She's the Blessed Mother. She never does nothing mean."

Guinevere turned away from them somewhat and sat staring strangely in front of her. Jennie and Tootsie exchanged slightly nervous glances. Jennie's stomach rumbled loudly.

"Gee, Gwen," she murmured, "I'm getting awful hungry. Do you think she would mind if you added hot dogs to the order?"

"Oh, Jennie!" Tootsie gasped.

In the house below Jennie's mother was making coffee, dripping hot water slowly through the grounds, as the French do, a somewhat tedious but thoroughly rewarding process. Through the double window over the sink she could see her daughter and her friends lounging on the hill, apparently deep in conversation. What do girls that age talk about, anyway? Surely not boys already? Jennie's mother bit off a fingernail, thereby ruining a perfectly good manicure. She had hidden away in a closet a carefully selected pile of books and pamphlets illustrated cheerfully in primary colors against the day when Jennie would start asking *those* questions. Psychologists in magazines and at Mothers' Club meetings always warned against the dangers of having *those* questions answered by classmates rather than in the proper, healthy way laid out in the books and pamphlets. She certainly didn't want Jennie getting the "wrong idea," whatever that was. Maybe she ought to investigate, discreetly supervise the children's conversation. But she didn't know how she could manage that without seeming to butt in. She hadn't realized when she had Jennie what a terribly complicated and difficult business it was to raise a child properly. But at least she could comfort herself that she was doing everything to bring Jennie up in the right way, not like the Italian child, the fruit of uncontrolled passion, brought up more on instinct than any book, nor like poor little Guinevere, no better than a foundling brought up by strangers in an institution. It was really too bad Jennie was so careless and willful in her choice of friends. There were so many nice children of good families living in Frenchmen's Bay.

After pouring out a cup of rich black coffee, Jennie's mother took from the refrigerator a half grapefruit, allowed by her Foolproof Ten-Day Wonder Diet in the middle of the morning. Beside the grapefruit in the glass and aluminum fruit drawer of the refrigerator lay a half dozen lemons. Ah, the perfect excuse for interrupting a potentially dangerous *tête-à-tête*. She'd make them a pitcher of lemonade. She bundled the lemons out onto the kitchen table, closing the refrigerator door carelessly with her foot. The door didn't catch, but flew open again behind her, and for some wholly unaccountable reason a package of frankfurters sailed out onto the kitchen floor.

127

15

In Spite of the heavy July heat it was cool in Monsignor Fulham's office. A large electric fan which sat on the filing cabinet opposite his desk oscillated in a languid half circle, spreading its egalitarian breeze throughout the room. Monsignor Fulham sat tapping his pencil on the worn Baltimore Catechism in front of him. The child sitting at the corner of the desk leaned forward, eager with the request the priest could no longer evade.

"Why can't I make my First Communion now, Father? I know it all."

And so she did. He'd tried every loaded question beloved of examiners. He could not trip her up. And yet Monsignor Fulham was reluctant to take the next step.

"Yes, Guinevere," he said gently. "You do know all the answers in the Catechism, but I wonder how much you really understand—"

"I understand as much as Aida Palmisano. Try me. Ask me anything."

Monsignor Fulham sighed. He was groping for some flaw in the child's innocent strength. He had carefully avoided any mention during their long catechetical sessions of the question so often on his mind. Things had been so peaceful and un-complicated lately, he hated to stir up whatever was lying dor-mant and destroy perhaps forever the serenity that permeated life in the convent. But now he felt it his duty to bring the matter up again. He cleared his throat and thumbed through the Catechism, seeking inspiration.

"Well, now, my dear. Before you make your First Com-munion, you know, you should make a general confession. Are you prepared for that?"

"Oh yes, Father. I've examined my conscience ever so many times. I've got all my sins lined up and ready to be forgiven."

"You're quite sure you've got them all? You wouldn't lie about it, would you?"

"Oh no, Father. Lying is an awful sin."

"Yes, it is." Monsignor Fulham moved in rapidly. "It is a very bad thing to lie. Have you ever lied to me?"

"No. I'd never lie to a priest. I wouldn't dare."

Monsignor Fulham paused, looking hard into the child's face. She met his gaze steadily.

"Good," he murmured. "Very good. Well, we shall see. . . ." He pushed his chair back and rose. "I wonder if Fa-ther Kelly has left us any Cokes."

The priest and the little girl sat at the kitchen table drinking Cokes from bottles. Monsignor Fulham allowed the silence be-tween them to stretch for a considerable length before he asked with studied casualness, "Do you still talk to Our Lady?"

Guinevere nodded, burping modestly behind her hand. "I'm not so busy now that school's out, so I go to the Shrine a lot. She's always there waiting for me. We have wonderful talks."

Monsignor Fulham managed to keep his voice steady. "What do you talk about?"

"Oh, lots of things. Stuff that's going on and about what people are like. I'm kind of dumb about things, so she tells me what stuff means. Like Jennie calling me a witch. You see, it doesn't really matter what names people use for things that happen. What's important is that they know something has happened. That's your problem, she says. You're afraid to see what's happening. She does want you to let me make my First Communion. She says you're afraid of that, too, but I can't see why. What could you be afraid of?"

"Everything, my dear child," said Monsignor Fulham. "Everything."

Guinevere sighed. "I do hope she doesn't have to make a fuss. She doesn't like to, you know, but she said she would if you forced her to."

"A fuss?" Monsignor Fulham tugged uneasily at his Roman collar. "What sort of fuss?"

Guinevere laughed. "Oh, nothing bad. She doesn't do bad things. Like I was trying to tell Tootsie, but Tootsie gets scared too. I don't know. But she did say she might have to startle you a little; that's not bad."

"No," said Monsignor Fulham. "I suppose not." He rose rather abruptly, knocking over his chair. "What do you say we walk out to the pier? I think I see someone crabbing out there."

The someone crabbing from the convent pier was Giuseppe Verdi Palmisano, taking advantage of his day off. He had baited three large drop nets with scrap meat from the butcher's and had lowered them to the shallow bay floor, tying their lines to the pier. A round scoop net on a long pole and a galvanized bucket half filled with bay water lay on the pier near him in anticipation of a catch. Tootsie and Manny were sitting on the edge of the pier dangling their bare feet over the side. They all eagerly greeted the priest and his pupil.

"What's that, Mr. Palmisano?" Guinevere asked, watching Giuseppe fasten a piece of fatty meat to the inside of a drop net.

"That's a net to catch the crabs in, Bambina."

"Oh," murmured Guinevere. "Do you want to catch crabs? What for?"

"For supper," Giuseppe laughed. "We want to catch lots and lots of fat blue crabs and take them home to Mama. She'll boil those crabs in hot crab boil until they turn bright red, and

130

then we'll all sit down and crack their shells and dig out all that sweet white meat. Ah, that will be some kind of feast, that is if we catch any."

"You sound pessimistic, Joe," Monsignor Fulham observed. "Having a spell of bad luck?"

Giuseppe shook his head. "It's just a bad summer, Father. Bad for everything." He raised his arm in a long theatrical gesture in the direction of the horizon. "It's all too quiet. Very dangerous, they say, a quiet summer. The birds and the fish, they can feel it. Why, we ain't had a good thunderstorm in better'n a month. It just ain't natural. The old folks say it's building up for a real whopper, a hurricane, even." He crossed himself and muttered, "God forbid."

Guinevere took off her shoes and joined Tootsie at the side of the pier away from the drop nets. Giuseppe smiled at the attractive picture the two children made, one so blond and the other so dark, yet dressed almost identically in playsuits sewn from printed feed sacking. Guinevere within the week after her visit to Liveoaks had been separately given two playsuits patterned on Tootsie's by the mothers of her two friends. Mother Ignatius had been a little uneasy about the modesty of the outfits but accepted them since even she had to admit they were an improvement on the gym suit. But she also decided it would be best not to let the right hand know what the left was up to.

"How's this little one getting on, Father?" Giuseppe whispered, indicating Guinevere, about whom he still had a certain protective feeling.

"Just fine, very well, really, except—except for this one little problem. You see, she . . ." Monsignor Fulham's voice slowly drifted into silence. No, he would not pass the pesky burden on to shoulders hardly capable of bearing it. Since Giuseppe was looking at him puzzled he was relieved to see Sister Helen advancing along the pier toward them like an angel sent to deliver him from temptation.

"Good afternoon, Sister," Monsignor Fulham called eagerly. "Come and join the crabbing brigade."

131

Sister Helen chuckled. "My senior girls would vote me president of that group. How's Catechism coming?"

"A little too well, I'm afraid," said Monsignor Fulham. "I don't know who it was decided this child wasn't too bright. She certainly has the Catechism cold."

"She's a phenomenal study, it seems," said Sister Helen. "Of course, she may be getting some coaching on the side."

"Hey, Papa, we got a bite," Manrico Palmisano shouted suddenly. He began pulling one of the drop nets up. Three large crabs were in it busily attacking the bait and one another. Manny and his father carefully upended the net over the bucket, shaking and prodding at the clinging crabs to force them to drop in.

"I think you've got another bite, Joe," Monsignor Fulham called. A second line was pulling as though it would break. Monsignor Fulham grabbed the long-handled scoop net in his left hand while he drew up the line with his right. The net was heavier than he expected, and he almost dropped the line. When he brought the net up to the surface he nearly dropped it again, for it was half filled with crabs crawling over one another, waving their feelers and snapping their big claws. Giuseppe brought the bucket over, but even with the assistance of Manny and the scoop net one of the crabs managed to escape and scuttled backward toward the edge of the pier. It was firmly halted by a plain black oxford set on its back. Sister Helen reached down and deftly picked the crab up at that crucial point on the middle of its back, where neither swinging claw could reach her hand, and dropped it into the overcrowded bucket.

"Holy Mother of God!" Giuseppe cried. "What's going on?"

He pulled up the third net. This one was full to the brim. Just as it touched the surface two crabs slithered off the top of the pile and plopped back into the water. The line to the first net, which had been returned to the water, was pulling again. Giuseppe stood openmouthed, holding the drop net over the water, unable to fit all his new catch into the bucket and reluctant to return it whence it came.

Monsignor Fulham began to laugh. "That's the trouble with miracles, Sister," he chuckled. "Our Lady in her bounty never knows when to stop. Here, Manny, you run fast as you can to the rectory and fetch the two scrub buckets and the big soup pot. Tell Father Kelly we're having a miraculous draught of blue crabs—good measure, pressed down, shaken together and running over. That'll bring him double quick." He sat down on the bench shaking with laughter. "From Thine infinite generosity, O Lord deliver us."

Giuseppe pulled the bucket toward him and gingerly transferred from the net as many crabs as he could fit.

"I wish to heaven I knew what this is all about."

"Gwen does it, Papa," said Tootsie. "She knows Our Lady. You know, really knows her. And Our Lady gives her anything she asks for like—like a grandma."

Giuseppe exhaled a long, sighing "Oh." His hand opened slowly and the net dropped onto the pier. Crabs fled in all directions. Some were recaptured, but most escaped back into the water. The girls scrambled up to avoid contact with the escapees. Guinevere came over to have a look at the catch. Giuseppe placed his hand on her head.

"Is that true, Bambina?" he asked tremulously.

"Yes, sir," Guinevere replied. She peered into the bucket. "Ooh, they don't look like they'd be good to eat."

Tootsie giggled. "They're luscious. Course you have to take the shells off. C'mon, Gwen. I'll give you a swimming lesson."

With the easy abandon of one who wears sackcloth, the children leaped into the water as far away as possible from the still struggling nets.

Manny came running up the pier carrying two more galvanized buckets, with Father Kelly panting in his shadow, a large aluminum stockpot clinking in rhythm to his pace. Palmisano father and son went to work at once silently and efficiently harvesting the heavenly bounty. There would be time later to marvel; their main concern now was the practical one of making certain that the gift was received.

"Well, Father," Monsignor Fulham announced, "you wanted a sign; here you are. Signs and wonders, all you can eat."

Father Kelly flushed. "I just don't find that amusing, Father."

"Oh dear," said Monsignor Fulham. "Don't you like our little miracle? I think it's first-rate. Or were you looking for something more spectacular—the sun standing still or the bay drying up?"

The buckets and stockpot were all filled to overflowing and still the nets tugged. Giuseppe dumped the remaining crabs back into the bay and drew in the nets. Manny, freed from labor, pulled off his T-shirt and jumped into the water to join the girls.

Father Kelly pointed to the incredible catch.

"How can you just assume that this is a miracle of Our Lady? It could as easily be the devil's work."

Giuseppe drew back a little, his eyes widening with fear.

"You have a point there, Father," Monsignor Fulham mused. "Too bad we don't have some holy water here. We could test it out. Nothing like holy water for chasing the devil."

Father Kelly reached into the pocket of his cassock and pulled out a small bottle with a black cork stopper.

"I always carry some with me."

"Ah, you must encounter the devil often in your work, Father."

Monsignor Fulham took the bottle, opened it, threw some water on the crabs and made the Sign of the Cross over each container. "BenedictusDominiPatrietFiliietSpirituSancti, Amen," he mumbled.

Both Giuseppe and Father Kelly watched the crabs intently for some seconds until they were certain that the blessing had disturbed them in no way. Giuseppe crossed himself a number of times.

"Santa Maria," he whispered, shaking his head.

"There you are, Joe," said Monsignor Fulham. "All blessed and ready for the pot."

"Will it be OK to eat them, Father?" asked Giuseppe.

"It is my opinion," Monsignor Fulham declared firmly, "that it would be a grave sin and an insult to Our Lady not to eat every morsel and enjoy it thoroughly."

"Here, Joe," said Father Kelly. "I'll help you get them home."

Giuseppe scratched his head. "Say, Father, we can't begin to eat all these crabs ourselves. There must be a hundred. And they go bad if you don't eat them right off. Why don't you take the ones in the soup pot, and maybe the sisters could use one of the bucket loads."

"Why, thank you, Joe," said Monsignor Fulham. "As you have not turned down God's bounty we won't turn down yours. Right, Sister?"

"Right, Father," Sister Helen responded.

Giuseppe called to his children to be careful and get back in time for supper. He picked up his equipment and one bucket of crabs. Father Kelly took up a second bucket. He stared hard into it a moment, then shrugged and grinned.

"Some miracle," he said.

"Yes," Monsignor Fulham murmured. He stared off unseeing into the horizon. Some miracle. Certainly more humanly appealing than thunderbolts and balls of fire. But it was disturbing, all the same. It all seemed too easy, smacked too much perhaps of Tootsie's grandma indulging a favorite child or, as Sister Helen had hinted, the capricious whim of the traditional fairy godmother. He wondered how the Church would rule on a claim based on so flimsy an incident. There were certainly some rather dubious things in the *Acts of the Martyrs* that had never been officially denied by the Church but that he was sure no educated Catholic seriously accepted as fact. But here this was, a wonder certainly, and he had been witness to it. The major question he wanted to ask now was not so much "if" as "why." After all, one load of crabs could be seen as a simple act of benevolence. An overload was surely something else. A sign? For whose benefit? Not Father Kelly's, certainly. It just wasn't Father Kelly's sort of miracle. It occurred to Monsignor Fulham that he might be the target of this particular manifestation. He found the idea very disquieting.

"Coming, Monsignor?" Sister Helen lifted the remaining crab-laden bucket and followed Giuseppe and Father Kelly as they carried their loads down the pier chattering like enchanted children confronted by a gingerbread house. Monsignor Fulham heaved up the stockpot laden with blessings and hurried to catch up with Sister Helen.

"You surprise me, Father," Sister Helen remarked as she walked down the pier beside him. "I hardly expected you to swallow all this whole."

"I haven't swallowed anything, Sister," Monsignor Fulham replied. "Let us say that I have been a little, er, startled. That is all. I have been blessed, or perhaps cursed, with a good deal of healthy skepticism. I take it you are unimpressed with Guinevere's miracles."

Sister Helen shrugged. "Nothing has happened yet that can't be easily explained."

"Quite so," said Monsignor Fulham. "But then I have read many rational explanations of Our Lord's miracles that make perfect sense. It's a strange thing; when I am with you my skepticism is roused again, but in the presence of simple faith like theirs"—he indicated the two men now walking across the church pavement—"I become a believer, too."

"And now that so many believers are in on our little secret, how are you going to keep it secret?" Sister Helen wondered.

"You forget Sister Clementine's camellias," Monsignor Fulham smiled. "Our Lady has a special interest in them, and would not want them ruined by the pilgrimages of the curious. Joe has been trained in crowd control; he will be easily persuaded to keep our secret."

He held the convent gate open for Sister Helen.

"Well, it's a nice little miracle however you look at it. After all, the crabs are a gratuitous gift of God whether they arrived in such numbers because of a direct heavenly command or simply because God made crabs greedy. The Palmisanos are sure to enjoy their supper all the more because they recognize that it is a gift from God. And so it is, however you look at it."

Sister Helen laughed. "You ought to have been a Jesuit, Father. You really ought."

Monsignor Fulham also laughed, bade Sister Helen a good supper and quickened his pace to catch up with the two other men.

"Hey, Joe," he called, "is the Communion Dress available?"

"I think Aunt Cecilia in Pearlington has it," Giuseppe replied. "Her Barbara was confirmed last month. But we can get it back in no time flat. Who do you want it for, little Gwen?"

Monsignor Fulham nodded. "I think it's high time she made her First Communion, don't you? Could Lena take it up for her?"

"Oh sure," Giuseppe said. "Just have to take up the skirt and make a few tucks in the waist. We'll make her as pretty as a Christmas tree angel."

Monsignor Fulham lugged the pot of crabs into the kitchen.

"What are you smiling at?" he half snarled at Father Kelly, who was holding the door open for him.

Father Kelly shrugged. "I just realized that more than crabs were caught out on the pier today. Perhaps Our Lady thinks it's high time the child made her Communion, too. And as Sister Clementine says, what Our Blessed Mother wants she sure gets, one way or another."

"You like boiled crabs, Father?" asked Monsignor Fulham.

"Love 'em!"

"Good. Then what you want you get."

He marched into his office and slammed the door.

SISTER HELEN was met at the convent basement door by Sister Anne-Marie heading for the trash barrels with an armload of outdated geography workbooks. War and its aftermath kept the book companies busy producing frequent revisions of geography and history texts, a situation that caused Sister Anne-Marie to intensify her novenas for peace and world stability.

"Look what we've got for supper, dear," Sister Helen greeted her. "Fresh-caught crabs, alive-alive-o."

"Where did you get them?" asked Sister Anne-Marie.

"Joe Palmisano had incredible good luck crabbing from the pier. Enough for his little army and some left over for the convent and the rectory."

Sister Anne-Marie looked at the crabs and then at Sister Helen.

"Was Guinevere there?" she asked grimly.

"Well, yes, she was," Sister Helen admitted. "But that doesn't mean—"

"Oh, doesn't it?" Sister Anne-Marie snapped. She turned away rapidly, muttering, "Dear God, where will it end?"

Still carrying her share of the booty, Sister Helen followed Sister Anne-Marie around the rear of the convent building. They walked together in the shade under the wooden veranda.

"Hadn't you better get those in out of the heat?" Sister Anne-Marie asked stiffly as she forced the anachronistic workbooks into an already overfull barrel.

"I think I ought to get you in out of the heat," said Sister Helen gently. "You look a bit green under the gills."

"Can I help it if I can't stand the sight of crabs?" Sister Anne-Marie snapped, slamming the lid onto the barrel in a futile attempt to mash down its load. She looked hard for a moment at Sister Helen. "Doesn't it make you at all uneasy?"

"No," Sister Helen said. "But then I like crabs."

"Don't you wonder what's going to show up next?" Sister Anne-Marie persisted. "I suppose you heard about Jennie's hot dogs. Maybe the next little blessing will be something less to everyone's liking. What then?"

"If it's nasty we'll blame it on the devil," Sister Helen grinned.

"That's not funny," said Sister Anne-Marie. "This whole

thing is getting less and less funny all the time. I just don't like it."

She turned back toward the side door. With a little sigh Sister Helen followed. She was sorry to see her friend so upset, but she had been warned of the danger of wishing for something so complex and elusive as Truth. It was a more admirable request than a sausage but likely to be harder to get off one's nose.

16

ON THE FIRST FRIDAY in August something nasty did happen. Frenchmen's Bay had a visitor, uninvited, unwanted and tragically unexpected. She was born in some unknown territory of the tropical North Atlantic east of the Lesser Antilles, and by the time man was aware of her existence she had grown large and strong enough to be given a name—Agnes, for she was the firstborn of the season. It was not a very appropriate name, that of a child saint christened in honor of the Lamb of God. She was neither gentle nor childlike and had no mercy. Men, helpless to deflect or destroy her, could only watch her approach with the desperate hope of somehow avoiding her. As a tropical storm she sailed slowly northwestward, feeding upon the unpredictable ocean's winds until she had matured into a hurricane. She slithered flirtatiously between the southern Bahamas and Cuba, brushed lightly past the Florida Keys and then veered suddenly northward, traveling diagonally across the Gulf of Mexico at only fifteen miles an hour but carrying near her center winds of over one hundred miles an hour. Florida breathed relief and Texas began to prepare shelters. The weather bureau warned everyone just to be on the safe side, for no one could be sure what the capricious creature might do next.

It was quiet in Frenchmen's Bay Thursday night, the sunset summer stillness, that brief-held breath before the tropic sun collapses, hovered over the little town. The water was as still as the air, a becalmed sea without a ripple. Inexperienced summer people from the city laughed and joked about the peripheral squalls they were likely to witness by morning as they hopped from the commuter trains which brought them from the New Orleans business day into the waiting cars of wives or chauffeurs (depending on how good their business days usually were). They smiled at the wily shopkeepers boarding up their plate glass windows. Evidently the natives hadn't heard the latest forecasts or seen the brilliant, nearly cloudless sunset. But there were no shrimpboats on the horizon, and the local police had been put on standby alert.

Giuseppe Verdi Palmisano, before leaving on night duty, quietly reminded his Maddalena that if things should start to look at all bad she was to close up the house and take the children with her to the convent. Although it was close to the beach it was one of the oldest buildings in Frenchmen's Bay. It proved its strength simply by having survived storms that had destroyed so many more sensible and more comely structures.

Monsignor Fulham stood at the end of the convent pier staring into the calm, his breviary drooping in his hand, for the Latin text kept being replaced in his mind by the mournful words of Coleridge's *Ancient Mariner:*

> *Down dropt the breeze, the sails dropt down.*
> *Twas sad as sad could be.*
> *And we did speak only to break*
> *The silence of the sea.*

As he watched, spellbound, the waters seemed to move of their own volition, for there was still no wind to move them, rising and falling in slow, strange, crestless waves.

"Swell," said Sister Helen, materializing unexpectedly on the pier beside him.

"Really?" Monsignor Fulham smiled. "I thought it looked rather ominous myself."

Sister Helen gave him the look she usually reserved for uppity seniors.

"What's the significance of the swell?" he asked.

Sister Helen shrugged. "Not much, really. It means there's a hurricane out there somewhere, but we know that already. It's no indication of where the storm might land."

Monsignor Fulham gestured toward the scarlet remains of sunset. "Red sky at night, sailors' delight."

"Whoever made that observation didn't live in the tropics," Sister Helen laughed. "But don't worry. That old girl is no more likely to make for land here than some hundred other places. And if things don't get too bad it's an interesting show to watch."

The show started at about seven-thirty Friday morning. There were squalls of varying severity all along the northern Gulf coast. There were very few places that suffered nothing. But the principal attraction, the lady herself, came ashore at midday, venting all the force of her accumulated passion on the quiet, clean little town of Frenchmen's Bay.

Mother Ignatius had taken the precaution of ordering a supply of canned goods and had the coal oil lamps brought down from storage. Other than that life at the convent that morning proceeded much as usual. It was best that way: six o'clock Mass in the chapel, seven o'clock breakfast in the refectory.

Morning chores were limited to indoor activity well away from windows—quiet activity like embroidering altar linens and hemming albs, while Sister Helen read aloud in her clipped finishing school voice softened by the memory of a drawl. She chose to read from a newly published volume of the poetry of Thomas Merton which she had recently acquired for the library, much to the annoyance of most of the other members of the community, who for the most part could not follow it. Sister Anne-Marie tried to listen intently, for she knew from the way Sister Helen read the poetry that it must be good. But Sister Stephanie made certain that her displeasure at the choice was known; she sat with ramrod

142

stiffness, occasionally sighing heavily and clearing her throat at maddeningly regular intervals. She was certain there was some infraction of the Rule in a brother of the Strict Observance writing poetry, especially poetry that did not rhyme. The wild ravings of the wind outside seemed part of a distant demonic world against which the room of sewing nuns was alone immune. But suddenly the outside world started to make itself felt. Mother Ignatius listened. There was a new sound that was not the storm or the wild rattling of the windows; it was a hard, insistent knocking. She knew at once that this was no demon knock, but a frightened desperate human knock. She laid down her needlework, signaled Sister Helen to go on with the reading and followed the sound to the upstairs rear door. A quick peek through a crack revealed Maddalena and the nine little Palmisanos clinging to the veranda. Mother Ignatius opened the door just enough to let them enter and then quickly bolted it against the demon. The entry of the Palmisanos brought with it the need to acknowledge the existence of the outside world and the peril that they all shared. Maddalena had heard an emergency alert on the radio. The hurricane had made a sudden hard turn east and was heading for the Mississippi coast. What they were witnessing, or attempting to ignore, was not the show at all, it was merely the overture.

The newcomers wandered into the common room, still dazed and shaken by their escape through the roaring wind and driving rain. Maddalena sat huddled in a corner, gathering her chicks protectively around her. Sister Helen attempted to resume her reading:

> "*Sun, moon, and stars*
> *Fall from their heavenly towers.*
> *Joys walk no longer down the blue world's shore.*"

Outside the demon roared and howled around the convent. The waters of the bay rose in great waves, pulling the sturdy little convent pier down with a splintering crash.

"Though fires loiter, lights still fly on the air of the gulf,
All fear another wind, another thunder:
Then one more voice
Snuffs all their flares in one gust."

There was a crackling sound; the lights fluttered and went out. At once the beam of a flashlight shone from the center of the sewing circle.

"We shall go to the chapel," said Mother Ignatius.

She rose and everyone in the room rose with her and followed her glowing light through the unnaturally dim hall.

In the chapel they recited the Rosary together. The candles glimmered comfortingly while the wind outside worked itself up to an hysterical screech and beat threateningly at the stained glass windows. One of the magnolia trees in front of the convent swayed and bent, then slowly cracked, making a sound like an explosion as it broke in half.

Panic began to invade even the candlelit chapel. Rosina Palmisano, who wasn't yet two, started to cry. Maddalena took her down to the kitchen in search of milk. Slowly the others drifted out of the chapel, to wander aimlessly about, not knowing what to do and incapable of doing nothing. Mother Ignatius went to look for a portable radio she was sure was around somewhere. Sister Stephanie suddenly thought of her relic of St. Martin de Tours and went up to the dormitory to find it. Sister Clementine sat in a corner of the chapel weeping privately. Guinevere came and sat beside her.

"What's the matter, Sister?" she asked.

"Oh, don't pay any mind to me, child. I'm just a sentimental old woman. I know it's sinful with lives in danger to cry over a graven image made by men, but I just can't stop thinking of Our Blessed Mother out there all alone in this."

"Oh, Sister," Guinevere cried, "you know nothing could happen to the Shrine with her there." She held the old nun's hand as she stared for a moment in thought at the flickering candle flames. "No," she said. "You're right. She shouldn't be alone." The child rose slowly and deliberately, genuflecting before the altar, and walked out of the chapel. Sister Clementine started to follow her, but then turned back and sank into the pew, clinging to her large wooden rosary for comfort.

Sister Anne-Marie stood in the senior homeroom a safe distance from the window, watching the storm. The wind seemed to be dying down and the churning bay was calmer. "Thank God it's nearly over," she murmured.

"Nothing like it, dear," said Sister Helen from the doorway. "The best is yet to come. This is just the intermission, the eye, the hole around which all these circles of hell revolve. It's after the eye passes that the thing really begins falling apart. And remember, dear, when you say your prayers, that this is what the insurance companies call an act of God. Makes you wonder, doesn't it?"

Sister Anne-Marie raised a hand to her face.

"Must you say that kind of thing?"

"Sorry, dear," Sister Helen said gently. "You mustn't mind me. I'm always facetious when I'm scared."

Something tugged at Sister Helen's veil.

"Here, stop that. This is my best veil."

"Oh, I'm sorry, Sister," said Tootsie, releasing the veil at once but continuing to stare at it in an effort to find some difference in it from every other nun's veil she had seen. "I just want to find out where Gwen is."

"She was in the chapel talking to Sister Clementine when I left," said Sister Anne-Marie.

"I've just been to the chapel," Tootsie said. "She's not there now. And she's not down with the others either."

"That's strange," Sister Helen said. "Well, maybe she went up to the dorm for some reason. I'll go see. We ought to stay somewhat together."

She ran up the stairs, not sure why she felt compelled to run. The dormitory was alone with its whiteness except for Sister Stephanie tearing up her curtained corner searching for the lost relic. Sister Helen took time to look in the other dormitories and the lavatory before returning to the second floor. Sister Anne-Marie met her in the hall.

"She's gone," she panted. "Out there, I think. She told Sister Clementine something weird about the Shrine."

Sister Helen looked out a near window. The calm of the eye was still upon them. A weak sun winked through the clouds.

"Dear God!" she whispered, not knowing whether the exclamation was a prayer or a curse. She ran down to the basement, opened the door under the rear veranda and stumbled into the wreckage of the school yard.

The ground was a swamp of mud that pulled at and clung to her shoes. She lifted the skirts of her habit and raised her feet as if walking in water. The shrubbery surrounding the Shrine had been badly damaged, and she had to pick her way carefully through occasional thickets of broken branches. A roar in the distance reminded her that the eye was temporary.

It was peaceful around the Shrine and relatively undamaged. Guinevere stood in her favorite spot, directly in front of the statue, erect, her arms uplifted toward the downward-thrust hands of the image.

"My dear child," Sister Helen cried, "what are you doing out here? This is a dangerous storm. Get back inside at once."

Guinevere turned slowly toward her. Her eyes were unnaturally bright but didn't seem quite to focus.

"Oh, Sister," she cried, "I'm all right. I'm supposed to be here. Nothing can hurt me; don't worry. But you aren't supposed to be here. You'd better go back right away. The wind's going to start again soon. Please go in where you're safe. Don't worry about me. I'm protected."

"That's crazy. It's crazy!" Sister Anne-Marie sprang up from behind Sister Helen, grabbed the girl about the waist and attempted to drag her back. She could not move her.

"Come on, come on!" Sister Anne-Marie screamed. "Help me. I can't move her. She's like lead. What's holding her down?"

"I'm supposed to be here," Guinevere insisted quietly. She appeared to be making no effort to resist Sister Anne-Marie's desperate tugging, but she did not move.

146

"I—I think we'd better go back," said Sister Helen, looking apprehensively at the bank of ominous clouds moving once more over the rising bay.

"We can't leave her here," Sister Anne-Marie wailed over the terrible roaring of the reviving wind.

"You must go back now," Guinevere declared firmly. "I must stay here. I'm protected. Go back and warn Sister Stephanie. She's in danger. Get Sister Stephanie out of the dorm. Quick!"

She turned her back on them and resumed her private communication with the statue. The rapidly rising wind beat hard against her, but she remained unmovable and unmoved. Sister Anne-Marie staggered back. The wind caught her, raised the skirt of her habit over her head and sent her spinning into the bushes. Sister Helen kept her balance by wrapping one arm around the trunk of a young mimosa tree. By stretching with her free hand she managed to grasp Sister Anne-Marie's flailing arm and pull her to her feet. They linked their arms tightly around each other's waist and pulled themselves slowly against the wind, clinging to trees, benches, anything more solid than their frail selves. The wind fought them all the way, throwing sea spray stinging like darts against their faces. By the time they reached shelter under the veranda they were wading in water above their ankles. The basement door was locked. Sister Anne-Marie leaned sobbing against the whitewashed wall.

"Come on, dear. We've got to get right inside," Sister Helen urged. Sister Anne-Marie did not move. Sister Helen seized her by the shoulders and pushed her up the wooden stairs, which swayed like a bad suspension bridge and nearly broke when a large piece of the pier slammed into them. The door and windows opening onto the veranda were all locked. Sister Helen tried to pull out a loose rotten rung from the veranda railing.

"Here, help me," she gasped. "It's our only chance."

Sister Anne-Marie, numb and distracted, obediently added

147

her weight to the effort. The rung snapped suddenly and the nuns fell back, slamming against the wall. Sister Helen stumbled to her feet, clutching the piece of wood. She had to hold onto the window ledge to keep upright, but with her second attempt she drove the rung through the window of the seventh grade classroom. She carefully pulled herself and Sister Anne-Marie past the jagged broken glass inside to safety.

As they stumbled out into the corridor they were confronted by Tootsie Palmisano, frightened and in tears.

"Where is she?" Tootsie cried. "Where's Gwen? She's not out there, is she?" The child buried her face in Sister Helen's wet and torn habit. "She'll be killed, she'll be killed."

"She would not be moved," Sister Helen said, stroking the child's hair. "She's protected."

Sister Helen hurried down to the common room, where the sisters were making an effort to continue with their needlework though trees and houses crashed around them and the roar of the lethal wind prevented most conversation.

Sister Helen glanced quickly around the room.

"Where's Sister Stephanie?" she asked.

"Still looking for her relic, I suppose," said Mother Ignatius without looking up.

Sister Helen made a strange sound and Mother Ignatius glanced at her.

"Good grief, Sister!" she exclaimed. "You haven't been outside, have you?"

Sister Helen did not reply but turned and ran up the stairs to the third floor calling loudly, "Sister Stephanie, Sister Stephanie, come out of there at once."

Sister Stephanie stood at her corner surrounded by her meager treasury of belongings: rosaries, holy cards, medals, various prayerbooks and missals, and a remarkable collection of handkerchiefs—the standard student Christmas present.

"Oh, Sister, isn't it dreadful?" she exclaimed. "It's like the end of the world, and me, I can't find dear St. Martin's bone."

"Come out of there, now. Please," cried Sister Helen. "It's dangerous. Come downstairs."

148

"Not until I find St. Martin's bone."

"No. Now!" Sister Helen ran into the dorm, grabbed the astonished Sister Stephanie by the arm and dragged her out into the hall. There was a sharp report behind them and a splintering sound. A tree limb as large around as a man's arm spun through the ceiling and slammed into Sister Stephanie's bed with such force that it split the mattress open.

Sister Stephanie sank back against the wall.

"My Jesus, mercy," she whispered.

"Come on, Sister," said Sister Helen quickly. "we'd best get downstairs. It's safer."

They turned toward the stairs but were blocked by Sister Anne-Marie, who stood white-faced, staring from them to the tree limb and back again.

"Oh no," she whispered. "Oh, God, no!"

"Let's go down with the others," Sister Helen urged. "We can talk about this when things are calmer. Do come on, now."

She tried to herd the others ahead of her toward the stairs. Sister Anne-Marie grabbed her by the arm and stared hard into her face. "Is this what you call an act of God?"

"We'll talk later, dear," said Sister Helen. "Just come down now, please."

Sister Anne-Marie moaned, then suddenly turned and ran down the stairs into the candlelit chapel. She threw herself against the statue of the Immaculate Conception, grabbing it around the perfect bare feet and shaking it.

"Stop it, stop it, stop it!" she screamed. "Go back to heaven, where you belong!"

She pulled at the statue as if trying to knock it off its pedestal.

"Sister! How dare you!" Sister Clementine rose from the corner of a pew and rushed at Sister Anne-Marie.

"You keep your hands off Our Blessed Mother!"

The full force of the hurricane struck the convent, shattering the stained glass windows of the chapel and causing the entire structure to shudder. The two nuns fell over each other, grappling and sobbing hysterically. The statue swayed, wobbled, tipped forward and then tipped back, settling after a moment once more erect on its pedestal. There was another burst of wind. The candle flames swayed, bent over as if falling prostrate before a greater power than theirs, and disappeared.

17

THE HURRICANE caught Frenchmen's Bay wholly unprepared. With only a few hours' warning the police and Red Cross attempted to evacuate the lowest and most vulnerable areas before the storm broke. There was not really very much they could do. When the wind began to rise dangerously, they were summoned with what evacuees they had to the new brick town hall to wait out the storm.

Giuseppe Verdi Palmisano paced back and forth the length of the auditorium where the refugees were assembled, drinking soup supplied by the Red Cross and listening to bulletins on portable radios. He had not had a chance to check back to his house to make certain that his own family had evacuated. Although he was certain that Maddalena would leave on time, he could not still his anxiety. As he moved about among the refugees, lending assistance and reassurance where needed, he surreptitiously fingered the rosary in his trouser pocket and tried not to listen to the wind.

Gradually he worked his way through the large room toward the rear exit. A plan was forming in his mind, a plan he knew was foolish and would involve him in an act of disobedience to his superiors. But he was by nature a man of instinct, and at critical times instinct easily took control of him. He slipped out the rear door into a hall and down a staircase to the basement. Here the rescue workers had hung their heavy raincoats and hip boots. Giuseppe had no trouble finding his own outfit and putting it on. He unlatched the door, stuck his head outside and looked around. The eye of the storm was apparently approaching; the wind had started to die down. Giuseppe pulled up his collar and pushed down his hat and slogged out into the mud, cursing himself for a fool even as he ran through the flying spray.

The wind had died down to a heavy breeze and a little sun palely illuminated the piles of rubble already accumulating along the road. Giuseppe had two bad moments as he slogged grimly through the stricken town, once where he thought he heard a cry for help from somewhere and again when he passed a small grizzled man standing in his shirtsleeves and bare feet in the center of a neat brick square that used to be the foundation of a house. There was nothing left but a toilet and an old-fashioned bathtub with lions' feet.

"It's gone," the man howled. "Everything's gone."

"You'd better get to shelter; the storm ain't over yet," Giuseppe called as he ran past. But he did not slow his pace, for instinct was strong in him and it was his own nest he sought.

His house still stood, if a little unsteadily, vacant and lonely. Maddalena had left and apparently in no hurry. The fringed shades of the two front windows were pulled down exactly three-quarters the length of the windows and were absolutely even with each other. It was a matter of pride with Maddalena that they should be precisely so at any time she was absent from her nest.

It was reassuring seeing something so normal. Fumbling at the top of the window ledge, Giuseppe dislodged the spare key and let himself in. The house was cool and smelled of furniture polish and oregano. Inspired by these homely odors, Giuseppe thought suddenly of the cherished gold cup that had belonged to his grandmother. That was an heirloom and ought not to be abandoned. He began rummaging around the kitchen looking for it, and even stopped to munch on some old bread sticks he found in a cupboard.

It was the violent rattling of the kitchen window that brought him to himself. The eye was nearly past and the wind was starting to rise again. Giuseppe ran out onto the back stoop. The three fine, healthy pecan trees that he had for so many years carefully tended and nurtured and harvested swayed threateningly around the fragile frame house. The storm wasn't bad yet. He figured he could, if he hurried, make it back to the town hall. The house was not at all safe to stay in. He leaped over the three back steps and ran, tripping over fallen limbs, his head lowered against the stinging force of the rain. He was running into the rising wind, and hard as he struggled, he seemed almost to be standing still. Giuseppe was rapidly becoming frightened. He thought he should have reached the town hall by this time. Nothing looked right. He bumped heavily into a tree; leaning against it, he tried to get his bearings. It was hard to see through the rain, but he realized after a moment that he was nowhere near the town hall; in fact, he had in his confusion run in the opposite direction. He was now somewhere in the Negro section north of the town.

There were trees all around him, tall spindly pines bending and cracking. Terrified, he began running again, first in one direction, then in another, looking desperately for shelter. He tripped over a root, fell flat and lay still.

The ground under him was wet and soft. Generations of fallen pine needles formed a thick carpet of decay. The storm was farther away down here, blowing over rather than against him. It seemed right to give up this terrible struggle he could not win and rest awhile here in his soggy pine bed. Giuseppe felt very calm and free from fear, although the sound of the wind above him was louder and his bed was rapidly becoming wetter. For some reason he did not mind these things; he was tired, and he just didn't care anymore.

Gradually, though, he became conscious of another sound, a

153

distant hum of bees, perhaps, or children in a playground. He rose on his elbows and listened. It was a pleasant sound, strangely out of place amidst the wild roar of the storm. Giuseppe sat up to listen better. The wind-driven rain struck him in the face like handfuls of hard-thrown gravel, recalling him as from a dream. Instinct and terror were aroused in him at once. He struggled to his feet with the help of a pine branch and began hobbling toward the sound, clinging to the trees for support. The wind pulled and tugged at his coat, almost tearing it from his body. His hat he had lost a long while back.

Ahead he saw what appeared to be a dim light. Then the whitewashed façade of the Harts of Love Baptist Church No. 2 appeared suddenly in his path. The light and the sound were coming from there.

Giuseppe leaned panting against the door and banged on it as loud as he could.

"Help!" he screamed. "Let me in. Please let me in."

He could hear a bolt turning. The door opened inward a few inches, revealing a youthful, suspicious brown face.

"Bless ma soul," drawled the young man within, a slight cynical smile on his smooth face. "The hurricane's done blowed us a white man. This here's a nigger shelter, mister. The white folks' shelter is on down the road."

He made a movement as if to close the door. Giuseppe pressed his weight against it.

"For the love of God, let me in."

A voice of quiet command came from behind the door.

"Let him in, boy. The wind don't know color."

The young man jumped back suddenly, causing Giuseppe to fall headlong into the room. There were a few minutes of confusion when he was conscious only of warmth and voices and the smell of kerosene lamps.

Slowly he became aware that he was sitting on a bench in the back of the little church wrapped in an old army blanket and sipping a mug of strong tea. Beside him sat Reverend Lucas, the church's pastor.

154

"Don't you pay any mind to our Jacob, Officer," he said. "He's been up North getting his brain educated. It kind of interferes with his soul sometimes, I think."

Giuseppe grinned. "That's OK, Reverend. I know how it is. I got a brother his age. He wants to change his name to Palmer so he can get a better job. It's my own stupid fault I got caught out there, and I'm mighty grateful to you-all for letting me in. It's getting nasty."

Jacob appeared before him, chastened and sullenly respectful.

"Ma would like to offer you some red beans and rice, if you want 'em."

"Sure. Thanks," Giuseppe murmured.

"We got a old wood stove back here," the pastor explained. "So we always ready for trouble, 'cause trouble gener'ly comes." He lowered his voice. "I don't know how safe this here church is in a storm, but it's the best-built thing hereabouts. I fetched everybody I could get hold of in here, and I keep 'em eatin' and singin' so they don't got a chance to be scared. It ain't much but it's all I can do."

Giuseppe accepted from Jacob a large bowl filled with a rich stew of red kidney beans ladled over a pile of long-grain rice boiled to perfection so that each grain stood on its own. "It's all any of us can do, Reverend."

The beans were hot and well seasoned. Giuseppe ate eagerly and began to take notice of his surroundings. There may have been as many as two hundred people in the church. There were several women in the little kitchen minding the pot of beans on the wood stove. A small knot of men whom Giuseppe recognized as the community's leaders sat together in a corner nearby, talking in low voices. Most of the rest, including all the children, were gathered together in the front of the church, clapping and singing under the pastor's guidance. It was their music that had roused Giuseppe from his bed of wet pin needles. The songs they sang were not the mournful slave songs and lamentations that Giuseppe had come to accept as the only Negro spirituals. The music that had revived him and that now comforted and cheered him was the music of joy and that freedom of spirit which belied both the singers' normally difficult lives and the danger that now surrounded them. The hurricane tore angrily at the little church, but the terrible noise of her rage could not drown out the gusts of ebullient sound challenging her from within.

> *"Rocka ma soul in the bosom of Abraham,*
> *Rocka ma soul in the bosom of Abraham,*
> *Rocka ma soul in the bosom of Abraham,*
> *O rocka ma soul!"*

As a hymn the song hadn't much to recommend it. It was short on theology and didn't make a great deal of sense. But it answered that afternoon in that place a need which neither reason nor doctrine could have fulfilled.

Giuseppe returned his empty bowl to the kitchen, thanking the calico-aproned women with their heads tied up in bright kerchiefs like caricature mammy dolls, and sat down quietly on the periphery of the circle of rejoicers. A young woman near him sang as she gave suck to her curly-haired infant:

> *"Mary had a baby, my Lord,*
> *Mary had a baby, my Lord,*
> *Mary had a baby, Mary had a baby,*
> *Mary had a baby, my Lord."*

Out of the corner of his eye Giuseppe saw something fly past the window. It looked like an uprooted pine tree. He turned from the window quickly and joined in the song, clapping his hands in rhythm:

> *"She laid Him in a manger, my Lord,*
> *She laid Him in a manger, my Lord,*
> *She laid Him in a manger, laid Him in a manger,*
> *She laid Him in a manger, my Lord."*

His voice was strong and well placed, and it rang like a bell through the little church. When the song finally ran out of even improvised stanzas and the singing paused momentarily, he realized that he had inadvertently become the leader of the chorus and the rest were all watching him. For one of the few times in his life he felt embarrassed.

"Good Lord, brother, you sing like a nigger," young Jacob shouted, slapping his leg.

"Oh no, brother," Giuseppe replied, winking at the pastor. "I sing like a dago!"

IT WAS WELL into evening before the storm subsided, leaving half the town of Frenchmen's Bay in ruins. The seawall and much of Beach Drive was broken into pieces. Water had flooded all the buildings within a half mile of the bay. The Catholic church and the basement floor of the convent were badly damaged by water. The diesel tanks at Ladner's garage had floated like toys up what had been the town's main street until they were finally deposited by the receding water in front of the Delta National Bank. There was no sunset that evening, only an increase in darkness unbroken except by the dull glow of an occasional kerosene lamp.

As soon as the wind died down Giuseppe left the shelter of the Harts of Love Baptist Church No. 2, determined with the help of his flashlight to try to get through to the convent. Failing to dissuade him from this still risky journey, Jacob offered to accompany him. Giuseppe firmly turned this down, reminding the young man that his own people were going to be needing his energy and courage, shook hands with him and with Reverend Lucas and started anxiously off.

He had trouble finding his way in the darkness, for so many landmarks were no longer there. Mountains of debris loomed up where streets and yards used to be, and he was forced to make many detours. One of these heaps of wood and trash, he noticed in passing without really comprehending, stood where his house and his pecan trees should have been. Once his flashlight beam fell on what looked like a human leg. Giuseppe hesitated only long enough to ascertain that the area had been flooded, and that no one caught under that pile of rubble could possibly have survived.

157

"*Requiescat in pace*," he whispered, crossing himself, and ran on.

He entered the convent grounds from the rear, observing with great relief the heavy shadow of the convent building standing in darkness, but still standing. In front of him was the shadow of the gazebo roof of the Shrine. The realization that it had survived the storm lifted his spirits. Going around the Shrine, he glanced back at the statue, for what reason he did not know. Sister Clementine's Blessed Mother stood on her pedestal, chipped and dirty, but very much all there. Giuseppe allowed his light to play for a moment upon her serene face, benevolent but not quite smiling, distant yet infinitely approachable. Then he saw lying face up at the base of the pedestal the naked body of a child. Giuseppe gave a cry as he recognized her.

"Oh God, dear God."

He knelt beside the body surprised, not that it was naked, most of the dead found after a severe hurricane are found naked, the clothing literally torn from them by the wind. What surprised Giuseppe was the lack of any sign of the horrible bloating which should have resulted from the body having been some hours in water. Her eyes were wide open but unseeing, and there was a barely perceptible smile frozen on her face. Her expression was indeed similar to that on the face of the statue. Giuseppe touched her arm. It was cold and stiff. Automatically, he groped for her wrist.

"Dear God," he cried again.

There was a pulse, very faint, like the pulse of a person in a deep coma, but very steady. Incredulous, he placed his ear against her chest. The heartbeat was not easy to hear but it was present. Quickly Giuseppe wrapped his tattered raincoat around her and carried her to the convent.

He hit the door hard with his boot and shouted a number of times before Sister Helen opened the door, extending a lighted hurricane lamp. When she saw him and his burden she quickly helped him inside, bolting the door behind him. She did not speak but looked anxiously into the policeman's face.

"She ain't dead, Sister," Giuseppe answered her unformed question. "But . . ."

"But?" Sister Helen whispered, studying the child's face under the lamp. "But what, Joe?"

"But—but . . . I don't know, Sister. She just ain't really alive."

18

THE DAY AFTER a hurricane is something like a lugubrious day after Christmas. There is little the survivors can do but look over their damage and try to figure out what will be left after all the rubbish is cleared away. The wind and the sea off Frenchmen's Bay were fairly calm, but the sky was still deep in cloud. The boarded-up shops that had withstood the storm opened to sell canned soups and Sterno at very high prices. The National Guard moved into the area about noon to assist in the cleaning up and to establish and enforce martial law against looters, the hyenas that always seem to hang in the shadows that surround a disaster's kill. A sound truck passed regularly along the few navigable streets calling for able men with axes and picks to search the debris for bodies. Sweating insurance lawyers searched the fine print of policies to try to find some way the companies could avoid paying for all God's acts.

Late in the afternoon Monsignor Fulham, returning exhausted and depressed from a pastoral visitation of the wreckage and its survivors, went into the church to assess the damage there. The floor fortunately was of stone and could be revived with a good scrubbing. The carpets and altar hangings, though, were beyond repair, and water had damaged many of the pews. Monsignor Fulham sighed as he looked over the shattered remains of his favorite stained glass window. If something had to be destroyed, he thought, why couldn't that nearly lethal tree branch have been sent through the miserable fresco above the altar instead of the convent dormitory?

Leaving the church, Monsignor Fulham went over to the convent, which had been converted into a temporary refugee center and clinic for the injured. There weren't very many injured, for most of the victims caught in a major hurricane did not survive the experience. Dormitory C, next to the lavatory, was relatively undamaged and large enough to serve as a makeshift hospital ward. Here Monsignor Fulham found Sister Helen, her sleeves rolled up past her elbows and her veil pinned behind her back, making good use of first aid training. With her he made a round of the beds, offering what cheer and comfort he could. In the curtained bed at the end of the row near the windows lay Sister Anne-Marie, asleep. Monsignor Fulham looked inquiringly at Sister Helen, who shrugged.

"Dr. Cameron's keeping her heavily sedated. That may not be doing her much good, but frankly, Father, we can't have her running screaming down the halls, scaring the children. And if she attacks another statue I won't be accountable for Sister Clementine. So I really don't know what else we can do with her until things settle down a little or she comes out of it."

Monsignor Fulham laid his hand lightly on Sister Anne-Marie's forehead and murmured a brief prayer to St. Luke, the holy physician. Sister Anne-Marie whimpered and rolled her head around as if trying to escape his touch. Monsignor turned to the next bed.

Here lay Guinevere just as Giuseppe had found her the night before, as lifelike and deathlike as a wax image.

"How is she?" Monsignor Fulham asked, somehow reluctant to touch her.

"Whether in the body or out of the body, I know not, God

knows," said Sister Helen softly. "According to Dr. Cameron, she is in an hysterical state brought on by shock. He makes no attempt to explain how she survived the storm."

"Do you make any?"

"No, Father. I've given up explaining anything. I know not, God knows. And Sister Clementine thinks she knows."

After a brief conference with Mother Ignatius and a look at the hole in the ceiling of Dormitory B, Monsignor Fulham started to make his way back downstairs. As he left the dormitory he saw something shiny lying behind the door. It was a small, flat sealed box bound in gold with one glass side revealing a tiny fragment of bone imbedded within. Monsignor Fulham kissed it and handed it to Mother Ignatius.

"I think this belongs to Sister Stephanie."

The basement had been somewhat cleaned out for the use of the homeless. It was filled with cots supplied by the Red Cross. Monsignor Fulham joined the line in front of a clinical table set up in the center of the room for the administration of typhoid inoculations. As his turn came he was aware that all the children in the room and some of the adults were watching him closely to see if he winced. He did not.

Maddalena Palmisano sat on a cot surrounded by her little clan. Her round, merry face had acquired overnight the hollow despairing look so often seen on the faces of women refugees, for she had lost her nest, the thing after her family most precious to her. Monsignor Fulham sat with her for a while, patting her hand and reassuring her that she would get all the help she needed. That was a somewhat hollow promise, for he had very little to give help with, and there would be many calling on him for it. But he felt he had to say something to relieve that unbearable distress. It was understandable that one sometimes had to resort to sedatives.

Gingerly Monsignor Fulham picked his way through the debris scattered about the convent yard and went down to the Shrine. Here Sister Clementine, oblivious to any greater need elsewhere for her energy, was clearing away broken branches

162

from the garden and the paths. She gave Monsignor Fulham an angelic smile.

"You see, Father, I was right about the child. She is indeed a saint, Our Blessed Mother's chosen one. Ah, we have been wonderfully blessed here, haven't we?"

Monsignor Fulham thought of the Palmisanos huddling in homeless misery in the convent basement and of the temporary morgue set up in the police station, where he had spent much of the morning helping dazed survivors locate their dead.

"Some of us have been blessed, Sister."

ON THE FOLLOWING DAY, Sunday, the sun came out, glistening in indifferent brilliance on the destruction. Church bells, at least the bells of those churches that remained standing, rang out as on every other Sunday of the year in a merry, dissonant rivalry for the souls of Frenchmen's Bay's faithful.

Guinevere stirred, as though roused by the seven-thirty summons clanging in a single insistent tone from the church of Our Lady, Star of the Sea. She yawned, stretched and slowly pulled herself out of bed. The legendary Palmisano Communion dress and veil, saved from destruction because it was on loan, lay neatly folded at the foot of her bed. It was the First Sunday in August, the day she was scheduled to make her First Communion. Guinevere put on the finery quickly, arranging the long embroidered veil as best she could without the aid of a mirror. On her way out of the dormitory she stopped at Sister Anne-Marie's bed.

"Wake up, Sister. It's time for Mass," she called softly, laying a hand on the nun's bare arm. "Everything's all right. The storm's over now and I'm going to make my First Communion."

Sister Anne-Marie shuddered and opened her eyes. When she saw Guinevere in her virginal finery, she turned her head and pulled her arm free.

"Go away," she cried. "Please go away."

163

Guinevere sighed and went away. Behind her all the length of the room she could hear Sister Anne-Marie sobbing.

The congregation assembled in the church was quite small, consisting mainly of refugees living at the convent. Most of those who still had homes to sleep late in would probably hear Mass at a more leisurely hour. Guinevere slipped unnoticed into a pew near the back.

With the electricity still out there was no organ, but somehow the thing was gotten through, to the relief of the celebrants and perhaps to the comfort of the laity, most of whom were as bare of worldly goods as that service was bare of ornamentation. There was a general gasp when Guinevere walked quietly up to the altar rail like an apparition of life in the midst of mourning. The other communicants moved back to let her approach first. She seemed neither to see nor hear anyone or anything around her. Monsignor Fulham was visibly trembling when he placed the Host on her tongue. Sister Helen, even as she bowed her head in wonder, had to admire the unconscious theatricality of it all. She should have thought of that dress for the final scenes of *The Wizard*. Very effective.

Breakfast, which took place in the big basement recreation room as there was no room in the refectory, was a necessarily informal matter. Guinevere silently took her ration of doughnuts and milk and ate by herself in a corner. Sister Helen, who was serving, started to speak to her, but decided suddenly that she should rather wait until she was spoken to. She had no idea what to expect and found herself somewhat reluctant to investigate.

It was Tootsie who finally broke through by the childishly direct method of walking over to her schoolmate and saying, "Hi."

Guinevere looked at her for a half a minute with a vaguely distracted expression on her face. She scowled as if struggling with something, then suddenly smiled.

"Gosh, hi, Tootsie. What're you doing here?"

"The hurricane blew our house away," Tootsie said solemnly. "We're among the homeless."

"Gee, that's awful," said Guinevere. The two best friends walked out side by side in silence. Guinevere turned to Tootsie with another bright smile. "But it's going to be OK. You're going to get another house and just everything you want."

Tootsie shook her head. She had overheard too much of her parents' conversations.

"I don't think so, Gwen. We got the wrong insurance or something, and the company won't pay. Papa's real worried. I hear 'em talk at night."

Guinevere grabbed her friend by the arm. "Everything's going to be OK, Tootsie. I know it. All I've got to do is ask."

Tootsie shook her head again. She had overheard grown-up conversations on other subjects as well, especially about the goings-on at the Shrine and Sister Anne-Marie's breakdown. She felt somewhat uneasy at the turn of the present conversation.

"Sister Helen told me you was sick," she ventured a little hesitantly.

Guinevere laughed, an unnervingly unchildlike laugh.

"That's silly," she said. "I haven't been one bit sick. I've been away, that's all. And I can go away again any time I feel like it." She leaned close to Tootsie's ear and whispered, "You want to know where I've been? I've been with her, I still am. I just come back when I want to or when she wants me to. But all the time I'm still with her."

Tootsie stared at her, wide-eyed. She understood quite well what her friend was talking about. She was frightened but fascinated.

"What's it like?"

"Oh, it's terrif, Tootsie. It's like the Emerald City and sort of like swimming under water and, gee, it's like nothing, just wonderful nothing forever and ever. Why don't you come with me and I'll show you? It's OK with her if you want to come, too."

Tootsie backed away quickly, caught by a sudden fear. They were walking toward the Shrine.

"No, no!" she cried. "I don't want to. Let's go back, please, Gwen. I couldn't go away from Mama and Papa. I just couldn't, really. C'mon, let's go back." She turned and ran up the path.

Guinevere hurried after her.

"OK, Tootsie, OK. You don't have to come. I just thought you'd want to. She told me you wouldn't, but I don't know why. I could figure Jennie wouldn't with her funny ideas. You don't think I'm a witch, do you?"

That caused Tootsie to slow her pace. She went back to her friend and took her hand.

"Of course you ain't a witch. You're some kind of saint or something, I guess. And I guess that's OK with you. Me, I'm just Tootsie Palmisano, and that's OK with me. Thanks for asking me and all, but I don't really think I'd care much for wonderful nothing. Look, there's Papa!"

She broke away and ran to her father, who stood on the muddy walk by the convent with the two priests. She clung close to him, holding his big hand tightly as together they went into the convent.

Guinevere walked directly over to Monsignor Fulham and looked at him with a steady expression in her eyes.

"Don't worry, Father," she said quietly. "Everything will be taken care of. But I'm afraid you're forbidden to get the church ceiling repainted. You must live with that picture for the good of your soul. Remember, it's not very pretty, but it's her."

She turned and walked back down the path toward the Shrine. Father Kelly stared after her.

"What on earth was that all about?" he asked.

"It just doesn't figure," Monsignor Fulham sighed. "You get all your miracles, with which you are never satisfied. But all I get is a reprimand. The mind of God is indeed beyond man's comprehension, Father."

Father Kelly shrugged. "I haven't the least idea what you're talking about. But, anyhow, the child seems to have come out of it all right. I suppose we'll just have to assume that she was just suffering from shock, unless of course she gives us some further sign."

"Further signs?" Monsignor Fulham laughed. "I should rather say they have gone quite far enough. I've witnessed all the wonders I care for, thank you. If you're really hungry for more miracles why don't you just ask for them? Who knows? Maybe she could come up with some new altar hangings."

He walked briskly back into the convent to see if he could be of some help to the indefatigable Sister Helen and to find out if there was any hope of having a quiet talk with Sister Anne-Marie.

19

FROM THE WASHHOUSE, where she was helping Sister Lucy try to get some of the stains out of the linen frontal, Sister Helen saw the limousine pull up in the school yard. She wasn't surprised to see it, for she knew Mother Ignatius had sent a telegram to Nassau, but she must have been somewhat concerned, for she crossed the rubble-strewn yard so rapidly that she was beside the car before the chauffeur had opened the rear door. The woman who stepped out looked haggard and anxious despite her gay peasant skirt and bright makeup. Sister Helen said as little as possible while escorting her to Mother Ignatius' office. She had no idea how much the superior had told this woman about her daughter's condition. She was glad, with all she had on her shoulders the last week, that this problem at least was being dealt with by someone else. Before returning to her work Sister Helen went upstairs to look in on Sister Anne-Marie, who was no longer on drugs since her hysteria had resolved into a state of quiet sullenness, but whose activities were still at times less than rational. Sister Helen found her leaning on the railing of the upper veranda, looking down on the parked limousine. Her head was uncovered and she was wearing a blue housecoat, all in direct disobedience to the Rule of the Order. She turned as Sister Helen approached.

"Now there's a fairy godmother for you," she said.

"I don't know about that," Sister Helen retorted. "She looks more like an ordinary mother worried about her child. But I do know you'd better get back inside before Mother Ignatius sees you out of habit."

Sister Anne-Marie laughed. "Who cares? God sees me. Maybe He'll send down a personal thunderbolt to strike me dead for daring to wave my sinfully beautiful hair in His sunshine. You've got to admit it looks lovely. I washed it with some special creme shampoo I found in the dorm."

"You'd better come in all the same," Sister Helen urged patiently. "There's no virtue in courting trouble."

"Oh, all right," said Sister Anne-Marie. "Anything you want, just so you don't send for the dear doctor to jab his needles in me every time I lift my head."

"I'm sorry about that," said Sister Helen. "But you didn't leave us too much choice. You were pretty hard to handle there for a while."

"Was I really?" Sister Anne-Marie grinned. "I don't remember much about it. What did I do?"

"Well, for one thing you tried to smash up the chapel."

"Three cheers for me," Sister Anne-Marie cried with girlish enthusiasm. Then she gave Sister Helen a keen look.

"Who stopped me?"

"Sister Clementine. I didn't know the old girl had it in her. She right up and tackled you."

"For that she should get a plenary indulgence at the least," said Sister Anne-Marie. She stopped at the doorway to Dormitory C. "OK, I'm back in the cloister and I promise I'll stay put. Now you just go on about your business and leave me to wrestle with my demons alone, all right?"

"I wish you'd let me help you," Sister Helen murmured.

"Help me?" Sister Anne-Marie burst out. "What makes you think you can help me? What makes you think I need your help? You want to do something for me? Just go on down to your precious chapel, light a candle and pray for my soul. Who knows, maybe we can scare up another hurricane."

Sylvia Simpson dabbed her eyes with the Kleenex proffered by Mother Ignatius, leaving a blue-black smudge on its whiteness.

"I just wish you'd tell me in plain English what's wrong with her."

"I can't do that," Mother Ignatius replied gently. "I don't know what, if anything, is wrong with her. She is in excellent health and quite happy, far happier than you or I will ever be. But something has happened to her, there can be no doubting that, and she has changed. I know I have been in the wrong not telling you honestly about this whole business from the start, but I think you can understand my reluctance to bring the matter up. Now, somehow or other, it's got to be faced. And you've got to decide what is to be done."

"But I don't know what to do," Sylvia wailed. "I don't understand what the hell—I'm sorry—what all this is about. If she's sick, I'll get the best doctors. If it—it's mental I can afford the best psychiatrists. But if she's really— My God, Mother, I'm supposed to be a Catholic, but I never really believed all those stories." She dug her manicured fingers into her scalp. "We've had all kinds in our family, alcoholics, drug addicts, things you wouldn't know anything about. But there's never been anything like this. I don't know what to do with this."

Mother Ignatius waited for a few minutes, her fingertips meeting to form a church on the desk in front of her. She gave the woman a chance to get control of herself. Then she spoke quietly.

"Have you seen Guinevere?"

Sylvia shook her head.

"Before you make any sort of decision," Mother Ignatius went on, "you should talk to her, see what you think of her condition and find out, if you can, what she wants. She's completely rational, you'd almost say normal, when she's amongst us. It's just that she's often, well, somewhere else. Why don't you go see her now? I expect she's down at the Shrine helping Sister Clementine with the cleaning up. After you've seen her yourself you will be in a better position to discuss the matter with me."

"Yes, I want to see her." Sylvia rose a bit heavily and started for the door.

"Please keep one thing in mind," said Mother Ignatius, half rising. "Before you think too much in terms of hospital and treatments, remember that she's comfortable and happy here, and we are comfortable and happy with her. As far as I'm concerned, she may stay at this convent as long as she wants."

SYLVIA ENTERED the ruins of the garden surrounding the Shrine somewhat hesitantly. There was a sound coming from within like rushing water: a fountain or a waterfall. As she peered around the bushes a small pool of water opened suddenly before her feet. She jumped back with a little squeal, then looked up as her daughter, dressed in a convent dress white uniform covered with a dirty apron, emptied a bucket of wash water on the ground in front of her.

"Guinevere! Good God!"

The girl laid down the bucket and wiped her hands on a rag hanging conveniently from the branch of a nearby tree.

"Oh, hi, Sylvia. I've been waiting for you," she said in an almost emotionless voice. She extended her hand. Sylvia took it slowly, allowing herself to be led toward the Shrine. Down a shaky ladder an ancient withered creature staggered to meet them.

"Sister Clementine," Guinevere addressed the apparition solemnly, "I'd like to present my mother, Sylvia Simpson."

Sister Clementine nodded a number of times. "Pleased to meet you. Very pleased to meet you." She pointed to a freshly scrubbed bench. "You just sit down and have a nice visit while I go get some clean water." As she passed Sylvia she gripped her shoulder and whispered loudly, "Don't you pay any mind

171

to what the others say; she's a real saint, that she is." She trundled up the path, banging the empty buckets together like cymbals to accompany her muttered chant. "That she is, a real saint, a child of God, that she is. . . ."

Guinevere took a seat on the bench, motioning Sylvia to join her.

"How come you were waiting for me?" Sylvia asked suspiciously.

"She told me you were coming," Guinevere replied, glancing up at the statue gazing down in indifferent benevolence upon them. Sylvia looked at the image and back at the child sitting beside her, trying to figure out how much of a change there was in her. She was so very quiet, not like a child at all. But then she had never known her well enough to be able to tell whether she was really quieter than she had been before. She looked well and her eyes were clear and innocent.

"Just what do you mean *she* told you?" Sylvia asked, trying to keep her voice steady and calm. She felt suddenly afraid.

"Oh, you know, Sylvia!" Guinevere exclaimed, a little impatient. "I told you in the spring. The Star of the Sea is my very best friend. She promised I could be with her always, and now I am." Her bland face brightened as with a great joy.

Sylvia winced visibly. So, there it was. Now she knew the superior was right. Something had to be done, and she knew what. Taking her child's face between her hands and looking hard and earnestly into the disturbingly clear eyes, she began to speak slowly and deliberately.

"Look here, honey. I've got a wonderful idea. I know a place, a—a sort of hospital. It's very nice, much nicer than here. They've got gardens and places to play, and the food's just fabulous. You can have a room all your own, with nurses waiting on you hand and foot and—"

"No! No!" Guinevere leaped up, her face turning suddenly terrible with anger and fear. "You're not taking me away from here. I'm going to stay here. You can't take me away!"

Sylvia jumped up, grabbing her daughter by the shoulders.

"You can't stay here, sweetheart," she pleaded. "It's doing

172

something to you. Don't you see? All this isn't real, it's in your head. That thing's not alive, it's just a statue, a damn plaster statue!"

Guinevere broke away from her grasp, ran to the center of the Shrine and addressed the statue, sobbing:

"Show her. You promised you'd show her if it was the only way. Now you've got to do it or she'll take me away."

She wrapped her arms around the hem of the statue's robe, and with a great deal of difficulty began clambering up the pedestal.

"Hey!" Sylvia shouted. "Come down from there. You're going to fall and break your neck."

She started toward the statue but stopped with a choked cry. She thought she saw Guinevere, kneeling on the edge of the pedestal, reach up with one hand toward the outstretched open palm of the statue's hand. When she was just able to touch fingertips with it, the plaster hand closed gently on the human hand and the statue drew, or seemed to draw, the living child to it.

"God have mercy," Sylvia cried. "I am a sinful woman."

"You are not!" Guinevere exclaimed indignantly, jumping down and pulling her mother back to the bench. "You're not bad, she says you're not. You may have pleased yourself but you haven't gone out to hurt other people. That's the next best thing to being good, see?"

"I've wasted my life," Sylvia moaned. "I'm worth nothing. But that's all over now. I'm done with my past. From now on I'm changed. I'm going to give my life to God. I'm going to enter the convent."

Guinevere burst out laughing. "Oh, don't be silly. You couldn't become a nun. They get up early every morning and wear black stockings and no makeup. You'd make a terrible nun. They'd throw you out in a week."

"You see?" Sylvia said. "I can't do anything. I'm worthless, God help me." She began sobbing again.

Guinevere sighed showily. "If you'll quiet down a little I'll tell you what you are worth," she explained patiently, as if

173

calming an excited child. "Just 'cause you'd make a lousy nun doesn't mean you can't do anything. There's so much to be done here and you're the only one I know who really is worth something."

"What in the name of heaven am I worth?" Sylvia whimpered.

"I think you're worth close to a million, aren't you?"

Sylvia looked at her daughter, a little shocked at the bluntness of the reply and anxious to be sure she hadn't misunderstood her meaning.

"Don't you see?" Guinevere persisted. "You've got what folks around here need most right now—money. Look, my best friend, Tootsie's house blew away. They've got nine kids and no place to sleep. There's a big hole in the convent roof, and Mother Ignatius doesn't know where the money's coming from to get it fixed before school starts. A lot of the stuff in the church is ruined, and there's all kinds of poor people in the town that need help. And of course Sister Clementine needs a new statue, but not right away, or she wouldn't have anything more to live for."

Sylvia shook her head. "You lost me a while ago. But I'll do anything she, you, I don't know, anybody wants."

"Great. She said you would. Now this is what she wants you to do. Go right to Mother Ignatius and tell her what's happened and let her have all the money she wants. I don't know, I think you can make some kind of thing with the bank, can't you?"

Sylvia nodded, calm, if somewhat grim with virtue. "And then what should I do?"

"That's all. After that you can go off and do what you want. Go to that south sea place and dance with your boyfriend, if that's what you want."

"But, but, what about you?"

Guinevere laughed. "I'm staying here, of course. But that's none of your affair now. Look, we both know I was always in the way. But now I'm taken care of, so you don't have to bother about me anymore."

174

"But that can't be right," Sylvia objected weakly. "I'm supposed to be your mother."

"I guess that's not your fault," Guinevere said with a light little laugh. "It's not so bad really, is it, to buy your freedom and go on your way?"

"Surely that can't be what God wants," said Sylvia, still incredulous.

"It says in the Catechism," Guinevere explained patiently, "that God made us to be happy. Now, you're happy in Nassau and I'm happy here. You need a kid like you need a hole in your head. And I've got a swell mother. OK? Now run along and fix it up with Mother Ignatius. I've got a lot to talk to my Blessed Mother about. Good-bye, Sylvia. Have lots of fun."

"Good-bye, honey. You be happy now. And if you ever change your mind, let me know."

Sylvia looked up uncertainly at the plaster statue, then gave her daughter a hasty farewell embrace in which there was no show of sentiment though neither expected to ever see the other again, and hurried back up the path to the convent to make arrangements for her final release from a burden not to her liking before heaven changed its capricious mind.

Sister Clementine, who had been watching the path from the diminished grove of trees that still somewhat camouflaged the washhouse, waited until the woman had gone by before taking up her bucket of rinse water and returning to her work. She had lived so long under the shadow of her beloved Blessed Mother of the Shrine that she knew every bump and crack in her. So it was no wonder that she noticed the subtle change in expression, the very slight suggestion of a frown that hovered about the painted mouth, an alteration that not even the ravages of the hurricane had been able to produce.

"What's wrong with Our Blessed Mother?" she asked Guinevere as the child joined her, scrub brush in hand.

"I think she's a little put out because I made her show herself," Guinevere explained. "She didn't want to do that. But it'll be all right. Sylvia isn't likely to blab."

Sister Clementine sloshed her water over the cement platform. "I don't see why she should get all that riled up about it," she mused. "After all, it's the sort of thing everybody expects her to do."

For an instant the frown deepened on the statue's placid face and then slowly relaxed into its familiar half-smile as the foster child of her choice clambered once more up the pedestal to rinse the folds of the formless bodice. After all, this was not the first time, nor would it be the last time, she gave in a bit and did what men and Gods expected of her in order to get what she wanted. Mothers had to work that way.

As Sylvia entered the superior's office bristling with new-found virtue and anxious to do good, Mother Ignatius asked her to be seated.

"I'll be with you in a moment. Please excuse me while I complete this letter to go out in the afternoon mail."

The letter Mother Ignatius was so anxious to get off was in answer to a rather unusual request she had received that morning from her provincial for a bilingual sister who would be able to teach English at a school for upper-class girls in the outskirts of Paris.

20

THE INSURANCE COMPANIES, in the manner of their kind, fought with every legal tool they had to avoid paying for hurricane damage. And although the storm called Agnes was declared an official disaster, government funds were predictably slow in getting to those who needed them. But repairs proceeded on schedule at the Convent of the Holy Innocents. Mother Ignatius as executor of what she somewhat cynically referred to as her Star of the Sea Discretionary Fund, got all repairs done to the church and the convent, bought a nice old farmhouse for the Palmisanos as well as assisting other dispossessed families, and had more than enough money left over to contract for the addition of a backstage area to the gym, a secret desire Sister Helen had not expressed even to herself.

By the end of August the convent was operating under fairly normal conditions and preparing as usual for the opening of the fall semester.

The school yard was filled with late summer sunshine, causing the freshly painted benches and bright new playground equipment to gleam like gems. Guinevere's jewel-bright voice floated out from somewhere back of the grove of trees.

Sister Helen walked around to the front of the gleaming whitewashed convent with a sprightly gait for one caught in the throes of menopause. The rural mail delivery car had just pulled out from the large mailbox attached to the convent's front gate. Sister Helen took out a pile of envelopes and quickly sorted through them. One was addressed to her from Marianne Brandon, and it didn't look like a wedding invitation. Sister Helen glanced quickly through the two hastily written sheets of blue stationery before she started back up the landscaped walk to the convent.

An attractive blond young woman in a light blue shirtwaist dress carrying a small suitcase was coming down the curved stairs that led decoratively from the front veranda. Now who was this? She didn't look like a student. It wasn't until she had come quite close that Sister Helen recognized Sister Anne-Marie.

"What are you doing?" Sister Helen cried.

"Trying to sneak away before you saw me," said Sister Anne-Marie.

"You—you can't do that." Sister Helen grabbed her arm. "You can't just run away."

"I can try," said Sister Anne-Marie. "God knows, I can't stay here anymore." She took Sister Helen's hand. "I'm sorry I haven't said anything to you, but I just couldn't bring myself. You're the only thing around here I regret leaving."

"Leaving?" Sister Helen cried. "You're not leaving the convent?"

"The convent, the Order, the Church. I'd leave God if I could, but He's hard to get away from."

"Oh dear." Sister Helen sat down heavily on the bottom step of the curving staircase. "I—I don't know what to say. I was just coming to show you this letter from Marianne. She's going to go to France this fall as a companion to Sister Stephanie."

"Splendid!" Sister Anne-Marie cried. "So she got hers, too: a one-way ticket, wasn't it? Since you're so happy to see her make her getaway, why deny me mine?" She sat down beside

178

Sister Helen. "I'm sorry, but I just can't stay here, even to please you. It just isn't in me anymore."

Sister Helen gave a short laugh. "Oh, I see," she said. "You've lost your vocation. Well, that's no reason for going out there. It's terrible out there; you don't know. You were so young when you came in here. Look, dear, you don't have to have a vocation to stay here. I don't have one, God knows."

Sister Anne-Marie shook her head, smiling sadly. "It's not just my vocation I've lost, it's my innocence. I know it's my own fault. You warned me against wishing for a glimpse of Truth, but I wouldn't listen. Well, now I've eaten of the fruit of Knowledge and I am sent from the Garden. Don't worry. I'll be all right. I've got to give myself a chance to think, to ask the questions I should have asked a long time ago."

"Have you talked to Monsignor Fulham?" Sister Helen asked eagerly.

"Oh yes, of course. I spent most of the week with him. He doesn't understand my torment either, but he has come to understand that I do have to leave, to get free of all this dreadful innocence, away from the Shrine and far away from that child."

Sister Helen bristled slightly. "And what's wrong with Guinevere?"

Sister Anne-Marie sighed. "There's no use telling you. You can't see it. If you could you wouldn't be able to stand it here either." She looked out toward the bay, gripping nervously at her skirt. "You like to remember the crabs, don't you, and the show with poor little Jennie breaking her leg. Nice comfortable little heavenly favors. But what about the hurricane? If this child and her Star of the Sea were responsible for one, who brought on the other?"

"A low pressure system southeast of the Leeward Islands," Sister Helen replied promptly, as if she might already have asked the same question.

"And dear Sylvia showing up to grant us all our wishes over the ruins of the town. Why doesn't she raise the dead while she's at it?"

179

"That one's a bit heavy, even for a fairy godmother," observed Sister Helen.

Sister Anne-Marie waved her hand impatiently. "Oh, you know what I mean. I just can't have any respect for a God who'd run his world like that, destroying a whole town for the benefit of a cheap piece like Sylvia Simpson. And Guinevere. All right, so you've fallen under her spell, too. But to me she's still just a rather dull, understandably neurotic little girl. Who is she, after all, that she should always get her way no matter who gets hurt? The Blessed Mother's spoiled baby! Blessed Mother! Maybe the lady at the Shrine is Sister Clementine's Blessed Mother, but she certainly isn't mine!"

She rose, looking expectantly toward the church parking lot. Sister Helen joined her.

"Oh, I suppose you have every right to be angry with God," she said. "I admit it all seems rather absurd and terribly unfair if you look at it at all seriously. That's exactly why I don't. Ah well, maybe you'll find your answers in the world. From my experience I think it more likely that you will find only more unanswerable questions. Once you've given up asking and learned to take nothing seriously maybe you can come back to the Garden, free from innocence and knowledge."

"I don't think I'd dare," said Sister Anne-Marie. "I have no idea what I might find."

"Everything as usual, I should hope," said Sister Helen. "Why not?"

"You're getting too mellow," Sister Anne-Marie said. "Can't you see what's happening? The cat's out of the bag. Sylvia knows, and even with the best intentions she's bound to blurt something out sooner or later. And you might not even have to wait for her to spread the story. The locals are getting suspicious. Haven't you seen the old ladies staring after Guinevere traipsing about in her white costumes? If there are any more little miracles around here, heaven help the camellias."

"Heaven help us all," said Sister Helen. "Or perhaps it would be a little more appropriate to beg heaven to stop helping us."

180

"Very good," Sister Anne-Marie smiled grimly. "That's the Sister Helen I used to know in the days before innocence. But what if heaven does stop helping? You've all gotten used to having your every wish granted. Can you adjust again to the normal human condition?"

"I hope so," said Sister Helen.

A large green sedan pulled from around the rectory and stopped on the parking lot near the convent walk.

"There's Monsignor now to take me to the station to catch the New Orleans train." Sister Anne-Marie took up her bag and started down the path.

"Wait, wait," Sister Helen cried, attempting to restrain her. "Think about it a little longer, please. It's such a big step. I mean, what are you going to do after you get out there?"

"I don't really know." Sister Anne-Marie gently extricated herself from Sister Helen's grasp. "I guess I'll just have to follow the Yellow Brick Road until I reach the Emerald City, or maybe just stumble back to Kansas. Monsignor's waiting, I've got to go now. I'll try to write."

"Can't you hold on just a minute?" Sister Helen fussed. "You don't have to go out there naked, you know." She began feverishly writing on a note pad she had pulled from under her bib. "Here are some telephone numbers, old acquaintances of mine in New Orleans. If you insist on going into the jungle it's a good idea to have some contact with the big cats."

Sister Anne-Marie took the proffered paper smiling. "Thanks. I'm sure I can use these. Good-bye now. Please don't come with me. I might start bawling." She held Sister Helen to her in a quick hard embrace. "You may pray for me if you like."

She broke away quickly, ran to the waiting car and jumped in. The car backed, turned and pulled out onto Beach Drive and was gone.

Sister Helen stood for a while in the heavy noon sunlight listening to the surf gently bumping the seawall. Then she turned and went into the convent. The basement floor was wet and smelled of pine oil solution, an odor that was soon overpowered by a pleasantly spicy smell that emanated from the kitchen. Sister Helen stopped a moment to savor the delightful odor of condiments frying in pork fat. Sausage. They were having sausage for dinner. She began to laugh. What was this? Another fortuitous coincidence or a new manifestation of the Divine Sense of Humor?

Wiping her eyes, Sister Helen turned up the stairs. Here the smell was of chalk and varnish, and in the chapel of melting wax and roses. Guinevere had been decorating again. Sister Helen took a candle, placed it in a holder and lit it. She knelt a long time before the altar of the Immaculate Conception. Mother Ignatius, entering the chapel for her midday devotions, observed Sister Helen kneeling with her hands over her face, her broad shoulders heaving just slightly. Mother Ignatius cut her devotions short, commending Sister Helen to her Master's care, blessed herself with holy water and tiptoed out.

The noon bell sounded hollowly through the old building. Sister Helen said her Angelus and stumbled out to the washroom to slosh her red face several times with cold water. Then she walked sedately downstairs to the refectory. As long as sausage was being served anyway, she might as well enjoy it.